He laughed n
say we're already about as up
close and personal as it's possible
for two people to get.

'But before I make love to you I would like to know *why* you're still wearing another man's ring.'

'I don't want you to make love to me. It's all been a terrible mistake. I should never have let things go this far.'

'Why did you?' he asked interestedly.

'Because I... I...'

As she floundered, he drawled, 'Don't bother to think up any lies. You let things go this far because you couldn't help yourself. You want to go to bed with me.'

Dear Reader

As Mills & Boon celebrate their centenary in 2008, this is a great time to acknowledge how much pleasure and romance they have brought to their readers worldwide, and to say a big 'thank you' for the small part they have allowed me to play in their success.

It's over fifteen years since they accepted my first story, and I was warmly welcomed into the fold. Since then, backed by a wonderful team of dedicated people, I've written thirty-five books for Mills & Boon, and had a great deal of fun and excitement doing it.

I always choose locations that I know, and that mean a lot to me, and I have to confess that, although I'm very happily married, I always fall a little in love with my current hero. I particularly enjoyed writing my latest book, MISTRESS AGAINST HER WILL, and I hope that you will enjoy reading it just as much.

Love

Lee Wilkinson

MISTRESS
AGAINST HER WILL

BY
LEE WILKINSON

MILLS & BOON™
Pure reading pleasure

First published in Great Britain 2008
Harlequin Mills & Boon Limited,
Eton House, 18-24 Paradise Road, Richmond, Surrey TW9 1SR

© Lee Wilkinson 2008

ISBN: 978 0 263 86446 5

Set in Times Roman 10¼ on 12¼ pt
01-0708-50047

Printed and bound in Spain
by Litografia Rosés, S.A., Barcelona

Lee Wilkinson lives with her husband in a three-hundred-year-old stone cottage in a Derbyshire village, which most winters gets cut off by snow. They both enjoy travelling, and recently, joining forces with their daughter and son-in-law, spent a year going round the world 'on a shoestring' while their son looked after Kelly, their much loved German shepherd dog. Her hobbies are reading and gardening, and holding impromptu barbecues for her long-suffering family and friends.

Recent titles by the same author:

THE PADOVA PEARLS
WIFE BY APPROVAL
THE BEJEWELLED BRIDE

CHAPTER ONE

IT WAS early, barely seven twenty-five, and London's morning traffic was still flowing fairly freely as Paul's pale blue Jaguar purred towards the city centre.

Normally, Gail knew, he would have been enjoying a leisurely breakfast before embarking on the day's business meetings. Judging by the look on his fair, handsome face, having his routine disrupted did nothing to improve his temper.

Sitting in the front passenger seat beside him, she sighed. She had told him more than once that she could make her own way to Jenson Lorenson's prestigious London offices. But, in spite of earliness of the hour and the personal inconvenience, he had insisted on picking her up and driving her there himself.

He had arrived early and, stressed and harassed when she'd changed handbags at the last minute, she had omitted to pick up her notecase. All she had with her was her purse, which contained her credit card and some small change.

When she mentioned the oversight to Paul, he said irritably, 'I don't see what you're worrying about. You won't need it.'

Perhaps he was right. With a bit of luck there would be just about enough to get a bus back home.

'Now don't look flustered, whatever you do,' he instructed

her as they stopped for a red light. 'Lorenson expects his personal staff to be cool and efficient. You've let this thing get to you and, now the crunch has come, you'll need to keep your composure.'

After a sleepless night, she felt washed out and on edge and in no mood to be preached to. 'I just wish there was some other way to achieve what you want,' she blurted out desperately. 'I hate all this lying and scheming.'

'There's no need to tell a lot of lies; in fact it's much safer to stick to the truth whenever possible. Your working background is solid and reliable, and you've got all the qualifications and experience Lorenson's looking for.

'Added to that, you've been recommended by a woman he trusts, so there's no reason for him to suspect anything. All you have to do is forget that we two have ever met and you can't go wrong.'

Glancing at her, he added, 'By the way, you did remember to take off your ring?'

'Yes.' The three stone diamond engagement ring that Paul had bought her was on a thin gold chain around her neck.

'Don't forget to emphasize that you have no ties and there's no current boyfriend. Lorenson has a massive office complex in Manhattan and he likes his Personal Assistant to be free and unencumbered, to be able to travel to his New York offices with him at the drop of a hat.'

'Oh, but I—'

'He's not an easy man to work for like Randall was. You'll have to be prepared for someone cold and arrogant and uncaring. Someone who expects his staff to jump when he says jump.'

'How do you know all this?'

'My sister, Julie, made a point of getting to know the woman who used to be Lorenson's PA. Apparently she'd been with him for over five years, and would still be working for him now if she wasn't planning to get married…'

As the lights changed to green, he went on, 'She told Julie that though he expects a twenty-four hour commitment, she rates him as a good boss…'

'When you say a twenty-four hour commitment,' Gail began uneasily, 'you don't think he'll…?'

'No, there'll be no funny business. Lorenson isn't known for mixing work and pleasure. Quite the opposite, in fact.'

'Then he's married?'

'No, and never has been. His ex-PA, who admitted she'd once been madly in love with him, told Julie she's convinced that there's no real place in his life for a woman.

'However, he's a good-looking devil,' Paul admitted grudgingly, 'and it appears that when he wants a woman to warm his bed there are always plenty only too willing to jump in with him. So you've nothing to fear on that score.

'Once you've got the job, all you have to do is be your normal efficient self and everything should be plain sailing.'

Gail wasn't convinced by his blasé attitude. 'But even if I *do* get it I'll be new, an unknown quantity. He may not trust me with—'

'The word is,' Paul broke in, his blue eyes impatient, 'that once he's chosen his personal staff he trusts them. He won't hire someone he doesn't trust. So you shouldn't have any trouble on that score…'

Somehow, knowing that only made her feel worse.

Oblivious to her mental discomfort, Paul was going on, 'I've had a report from someone I'd already planted—the plans for the Rainmaker project should be finalized in the next few weeks, which means we're just in the nick of time.

'As soon as you've managed to see those plans and get the latest gen, just let me know.'

He made the whole thing sound so casual, so innocuous, Gail thought helplessly, but to her it was spying, pure and simple, and she hated the thought of being involved.

But after days of unrelenting pressure Paul had made it a test of her love....

'There'll never be another opportunity like this. With his present PA leaving just as the Rainmaker project is going through, and you being out of a job, this is exactly the chance I've been waiting for.

'Lorenson has a reputation for being daring, for sticking his neck out when it comes to these really big deals. That's how he comes to be a billionaire at just turned thirty. If he intends to play it the same way this time *and I know about it in advance* I can be waiting with a hatchet.

'This is important to me.' He took her hand and squeezed it by way of emphasis. 'I have to know what's in those plans. I need to be at least one jump ahead.' Taking her hand to his lips and pressing a kiss to her palm he continued, 'That way, if I can't bring him down altogether, and he may be too powerful for that,' Paul admitted regretfully, 'at the very least, I can bring him to his knees.

'All I need is some reliable inside information, and when you're his PA it'll be a doddle...'

When Paul had first mentioned Jenson Lorenson, Gail had felt her heart stop, then start to race again uncomfortably fast.

'Jenson Lorenson?' she echoed warily.

'Don't tell me you've never heard the name. It's a big Anglo-American concern. It was started in the States by Richard Jenson just as the boom in electronics really got under way.

'When Jenson retired five years ago, he made the company over to Zane Lorenson, his nephew, who'd been his right-hand man for a number of years...'

So it was him.

Unbidden, a mental picture of Zane Lorenson filled her mind. Tall, black-haired, broad-shouldered and narrow-hipped... A lean, tanned face with strong features... A mouth like a fallen angel, and long, heavy-lidded dark green eyes. Handsome eyes. Eyes that seemed able to look into her very soul.

A shiver ran through her.

Paul went on, oblivious to her reaction. 'Lorenson, who had an American mother and an English father, is a clever swine and brilliant when it comes to business. He added the Anglo part, moved into Information Technology and Research and Development and trebled the company's profits inside two years...'

'But I don't see what—'

Paul cut in, speaking over her. 'He's an old adversary. That swine was responsible for my first company going down, and I've hated his guts ever since. Now, with your help, I've a chance to derail the Rainmaker project and get some of my own back.'

Gail turned to him, wide-eyed. 'With *my* help? Oh, but I—'

'Just listen. It should work like a dream...'

While he outlined the scheme her agitation grew. As soon as she could get a word in edgeways she said in a rush, 'No, Paul. I don't want anything to do with it.'

Once again, he dismissed her protest. 'It won't be difficult. Think about it. I'm sure you'll change your mind.'

'I won't change my mind.'

With a smile that would normally have melted her heart, he coaxed, 'Come on, sweetie, do it for me.'

Even if it hadn't involved Zane Lorenson she wouldn't have wanted to do it. But as it *did,* there was no way...

'I'd never be able to bring it off.'

Well aware that she was besotted with him, and wondering at her unusual reluctance to toe the line he had marked out for her, Paul demanded, 'Surely you could at least try?'

Her lovely mouth set in a determined line, she shook her head. 'I don't want to get involved.'

Paul turned to meet her gaze and said somewhat sharply, 'You once said you'd do anything for me.'

'I said anything I *could* do. But this is something I *can't* do,' Gail pleaded.

'Why can't you?'

She shook her head, helplessly. 'I just *can't*.'

'There must be a reason,' he pressed.

Cornered, she blurted out, 'I once knew him.'

'How do you mean, you once knew him?'

'I met him when I was living in the States. He was…friends with Rona.'

'Your stepsister?'

Gail nodded. 'Yes.'

'I thought you'd been back in England for quite a few years?'

'I have—'

Paul brushed off her concerns. 'So it must have been some time ago?'

'Seven years.' She didn't add that for seven long years Zane Lorenson's image had haunted her. 'I was just seventeen.'

'Did you know him well?'

'No…' In spite of what had happened, she hadn't really *known* him at all.

Awkwardly, she added, 'But we met two or three times and I—'

His face impatient, Paul butted in, 'When your mother remarried after your own father's death, did your new stepfather adopt you?'

'No.'

'In that case you and your stepsister must have different surnames.'

'Yes, but—'

'Then what are you worrying about? Your name won't ring a bell, and if you only met each other two or three times he's hardly likely to remember you after seven years.'

'But suppose he did?'

'If by any faint chance he did, would it matter?'

'Yes, it would… You see I—'

'My dear girl,' Paul interrupted peevishly, 'do you seriously believe there's a cat in hell's chance of him recognising you after all this time…?'

The honest answer was no. She had been less than nothing to the young Zane Lorenson. Until Rona had turned that cruel spotlight on her, he hadn't even been aware of her existence.

'If you really think there might be a problem, for goodness' sake find some way of altering your appearance; get some glasses or something.

'But I'm quite certain you're worrying over nothing. In the last seven years you must have altered a great deal.'

She had.

In those days she had been just a gawky adolescent, a late developer, painfully shy and gauche, and still with the remains of a northern accent.

Then, goaded by Rona, and hopelessly in love with a man she had only seen from afar, she had set about changing her image.

Only to be laughed at and ridiculed by her stepsister who, at twenty-three, had been beautiful and glamorous and worldly.

But that hadn't been the worst…

She pushed the memory—still unbearably shameful and humiliating even after all these years—away and tried to concentrate on what she had become.

To all intents and purposes she was now a cool, self-possessed young woman with dark glossy hair, a clear skin, a good figure, a polished manner and no trace of an accent.

No, in all truth, Zane Lorenson was hardly likely to recognize her.

But remembering how he had looked at her the last time they'd met—his set lips, the cold fury in those green eyes—she still didn't want to take the risk.

'I don't want to have to see him again. I'm afraid…' About to say, *I'm afraid of him,* unwilling to have Paul laugh at her, she changed it to, 'I'm afraid I don't like him. I'd simply *hate* to have to work for him.'

Paul's fair face darkened. 'I think in the circumstances that's a very selfish attitude. After all, it wouldn't be for long. As soon as you've got the information I want, you can make some excuse and leave.'

Her grey eyes beseeching, she begged, 'Please, Paul, don't ask me to do this.'

Such a heartfelt plea ought to have melted stone. But his expression hard, unrelenting, he said, 'It's not as if it's *that* much to ask, and you'd do it for my sake if you really loved me.'

As, hating that look of censure, the feeling that she was letting him down, she wavered, he pressed, 'Of course if you *don't* there's not much point in our getting engaged.'

'I *do* love you.'

'Then prove it.'

Finally giving in to the pressure, she agreed unhappily. 'Very well, I'll try.'

Triumphantly, he drawled smugly, 'That's my girl. I always knew you wouldn't let me down.

'Now just one thing, no one else must know, so don't say anything to that flatmate of yours. Simply tell her you've got another job.'

She looked across at him, still worried about the plan. 'I might not get it.'

'Of course you will. It's practically a cert.'

As a reward for toeing the line, he had taken her out and bought her an engagement ring.

With his red-gold hair and Greek god looks, his bright blue eyes and long curly lashes, the boyish smile that added to his charm, most women he came into contact with were bowled over.

Gail had been no exception.

He had called one morning to see David Randall, her ex-boss, and after years of thinking she would never fall in love again, she had done just that.

A small, privately owned company, Randalls had been highly successful, coming up with some brilliant ideas that seemed set to revolutionize their particular branch of electronics.

They had been on the point of putting the new ideas into practice when David Randall had had a heart attack which had made him decide to sell out and retire at the early age of fifty-five.

The Manton Group, which Paul owned, had made an offer for the company, but it had been a derisory offer in David Randall's opinion.

As the negotiations dragged on, Paul had become a frequent visitor, often stopping by Gail's desk to have a chat. When one day he asked her to have dinner with him, she had been both flattered and flustered.

From then on he had taken her out a good deal and, though he had been both romantic and ardent, unlike her previous boyfriend, he had made no attempt to take her back to his place or get her into bed.

This restraint, as well as his good looks and his undeniable charm, had set him apart and deepened her feelings for him.

Finally the business deal had gone through and David Randall had left the company he had built up single-handed, satisfied that he had negotiated a fair deal for his employees.

But, as soon as Randalls was his, Paul had paid off staff and workers alike and closed the company down.

When, badly shaken, her liking and respect for Paul diminished, Gail had ventured to protest, he had answered that all the employees had received a generous cash settlement and most of them had been quite content.

'But it isn't what David intended,' she insisted. 'He spent a lifetime building up that company. He regarded his workers almost as family, and he wanted them all to keep their jobs—'

'My dear girl, you ought to know by now that there's no sentiment in business. Randalls was opposition we could well do without. A thorn in our side that had to be removed,' he answered dismissively.

'That wasn't what you told David Randall,' she said accusingly. 'You gave him to understand that nothing much would change.'

Paul shrugged. 'It was business, darling. He may have chosen to believe otherwise, but this was the best decision all round, I promise.'

Seeing she was still far from happy, and needing to keep her on his side for what he had in mind, he pulled her close and kissed her. 'Now let's forget all about work. If you really want another job, I'll give you one. But I thought you might prefer to be Mrs Paul Manton…'

Paul wanted to marry her. Still besotted by him, in spite of all that had happened, she floated up to cloud nine.

'But before we start planning the wedding, there's something I want you to do for me…'

She had come down to earth again with a bump when he'd explained what it was he wanted her to do and, even with his engagement ring on her finger, her joy had been marred by the thought of what was in store.

'This job you want me to apply for—' she broached the subject with reluctance '—how shall I go about it?'

'Don't worry about that. I know Mrs Rogers, the woman who runs the employment agency that Lorenson uses. I'll ask her to see you and recommend you for the position.'

Gail had found herself hoping that for once in his life Paul wouldn't succeed in pulling strings and manipulating people.

But, with the kind of looks and charm that made slaves of the female sex, he had, and she had been asked to call and see Mrs Rogers.

The following day the agency had rung to say that an interview had been arranged.

Though pleased that everything had so far gone according to plan, Paul had complained bitterly about the earliness of the hour.

'Lorenson wants you to be at his office at eight o'clock! Why the hell can't he work nine to five like most people?

'Well, you'll just have to take care not to be late. The swine is a stickler for punctuality and you'll need to look cool.'

Then, with a thoughtful glance at her face, 'Perhaps I'd better pick you up.'

'There's no need to do that. I can make my own way there. I'll get a taxi if necessary.'

After a moment or two's consideration, he said decidedly, 'No, it'll be best if I come round and collect you.'

She had strongly suspected that it was in case she chickened out at the last minute.

Whatever his reason, he had picked her up on the dot of seven fifteen, so now here she was, on her way to be interviewed for the position of PA to a man she had hoped never to have to see again.

Talk about being caught between the devil and the deep

blue sea, she thought miserably. If she didn't get it, Paul would be furious with her. If she *did,* she would be in an invidious position…

'We're almost there.' His voice broke into her unhappy thoughts. 'Lorenson's offices, as well as his own private apartment, are in the Clairmont Building on Lower Arlington Street. But, just to make certain no one spots you getting out of my car, I'll drop you at the corner.'

When they reached their destination, he drew in to the kerb and issued his last instructions. 'Now don't forget, try not to look flustered whatever you do, or all this planning and preparation will be wasted.

'And don't breathe a word about me. Lorenson would soon be on his guard if he picked up any suggestion that we know each other.' His gaze held a warning and Gail looked away as he continued, 'When the interview's over and you're well away from Lorenson's offices, you can give me a quick call and let me know for sure if you've got the job.'

Gail hesitated, still uncertain and unsure. 'But suppose one of his staff is doing the interviewing and is just compiling a short-list?'

'According to Mrs Rogers, Lorenson doesn't work that way. The people he wants on his own staff he always interviews personally, and usually he makes an on-the-spot decision.'

Gail's heart sank. She had held on to the faint hope that it might be one of his minions she would have to see, and that said minion would prefer some other candidate, thus giving her a let-out. But it seemed it wasn't to be.

Urgently in need of reassurance, she asked, 'When shall I see you? Lynne will be out tonight if you want to come round for a meal.'

'Once Lorenson knows where you live, it might not be safe.'

Trying to keep the tell-tale tremor out of her voice, she suggested, 'Well, couldn't we meet in the park, or at a restaurant, or something?'

But, instead of softening, those eyes, blue as summer skies, looked at her dismissively. 'It's too big a risk. We can't afford to jeopardise our chances by possibly being seen together.

'After you've let me know the score it would be better if we don't have any contact until you've something to report.'

'Oh,' she said blankly.

'When you have, you'd better give me a ring at the office and we'll meet up somewhere.'

He leaned over and gave her a quick peck on the cheek. 'Now don't forget how much this means to me. Good luck.'

Feeling slightly sick, her stomach full of butterflies, Gail unfastened her seat belt, opened the door and got out.

Already the air was warm and the summer sunshine bright, glancing off the bodywork of passing cars and gleaming on pavements still damp from the early morning shower.

As the Jaguar drew away, she lifted her hand but, a slight frown on his good-looking face, Paul was staring straight ahead.

Opening her bag, she took out the pair of cheap low-strength reading glasses she'd bought in the local chemist and put them on.

Then bracing herself, she walked the short distance to the Clairmont Building, with its handsome Georgian façade, and through the imposing main entrance.

The clock above the reception desk showed it was ten minutes to eight, so she was in good time.

As, her heart beating fast and her legs feeling oddly shaky, she started to cross the marble-floored lobby, she caught sight of herself reflected in one of the long gilt-framed mirrors.

Wearing a smart charcoal-grey suit and an off-white blouse, her small heart-shaped face outwardly calm, her dark hair in a smooth coil, she looked every inch the cool, efficient business-woman.

No one would have guessed at her inner turmoil as she approached the desk and gave her name to the pretty blonde receptionist.

'You'll find the office complex on the second floor, Miss North. If you would like to go straight up, Mrs Bancroft, Mr Lorenson's secretary, will be waiting for you.'

When Gail stepped out of the lift on the second floor she was greeted by an attractive middle-aged woman with bobbed iron-grey hair.

'I'm Claire Bancroft. If you'd like to follow me, Miss North…'

As Mrs Bancroft led the way along the carpeted corridor to another lift, she remarked, 'Mr Lorenson is in his apartment this morning. He likes to keep the interviews he conducts informal.'

Entering a four digit code into a small panel, she added, 'This is his private lift.'

The lift took them up to the top floor, where they emerged into a quietly luxurious hallway. Opening the nearest door, Mrs Bancroft said, 'Please come in, Miss North…'

Gail found herself ushered into a large sunny room with an off-white and mint-green decor and an ornate plaster ceiling. To the left, a door into a neighbouring room stood slightly ajar.

Between two sets of windows was a desk with an impressive array of the latest electronic equipment and a black leather chair.

Apart from the businesslike desk, the room was furnished as a lounge.

'Perhaps you'd like to take a seat?' Mrs Bancroft suggested with a friendly smile. 'Mr Lorenson knows you're here. He'll be with you in a minute or so.'

When the other woman had gone, too nervous to sit and

cravenly grateful for even this short breathing space, Gail looked around curiously.

Along with some lovely antique furniture, there were a couple of comfortable-looking couches, several soft off-white leather armchairs and a large round coffee table.

A thick-pile smoke-grey carpet covered the floor and on either side of a beautiful Adam fireplace, which was filled with fresh flowers, there were recessed bookcases, their shelves overflowing.

Considering how very strongly she had felt about Zane Lorenson, aside from his appearance, she had known hardly anything about the man himself, what he was really like, what his tastes were.

This appeared to be the room of a man with eclectic tastes, a man who preferred his surroundings to be both simple and elegant.

On the walls several stark and dramatic snow scenes by Jonathan Cass rubbed shoulders with the vibrant colour and slumberous warmth of Tuscan landscapes by Marco Abruzzi.

Frowning a little, she studied them. With such diverse techniques and subject matter, they shouldn't have been hung together. But somehow the contrast worked, highlighting them both.

It seemed that Zane Lorenson was a man who knew precisely what he wanted and wasn't afraid to try the less obvious.

Her mother had always said that one could get a good idea of a person's character from what kind of books they read so, taking a deep breath, Gail moved closer to the bookcases and looked at their contents.

Classics and poetry, travel and adventure, mysteries, biographies, autobiographies, the best popular paperback fiction and Booker Prize winners jostled for space.

She had picked up a copy of a recent Booker Prize winner when, glancing up, she met a pair of brilliant dark eyes.

He was leaning negligently against the door jamb, his tough, good-looking face shrewd, calculating, an arrogant tilt to his dark head.

Wearing a smart light-weight suit, a crisp shirt and tie and handmade shoes, he looked every inch the billionaire business-man. He also looked fit and virile and dangerous.

Though she had braced herself to see him again, the shock hit her like a blow over the heart and in that instant her heart-beat and her breathing, the very blood flowing through her veins, seemed to stop.

She had remembered how he looked—of course she had, his face had haunted her for years—and, apart from an added maturity, he looked much the same now as he had then.

But in the intervening years she had almost forgotten just what a powerful impact his physical presence had on her.

While she stood rooted to the spot, endeavouring to pull herself together, he continued to stand and study her in unnerv-ing silence.

It seemed an age, but could only have been seconds, before she released the breath she was holding and her heart began to beat again in slow, heavy thuds.

How long had he been standing there quietly watching her while she'd nosed amongst his personal belongings?

She felt herself shrivel inwardly. Her one consolation was that the cool green gaze fixed on her face held no sign of rec-ognition. But she had known it wouldn't.

As soon as she had managed to regain some semblance of composure, she thrust the book she was holding back on to the shelf and said unevenly, 'I'm sorry; I was just…'

'Taking a look at what I read? What conclusion did you come to?'

His voice was low-pitched and attractive. It was a voice she had never forgotten. A voice she would have known amongst a million. A voice that could have called her back from the grave.

Shaken afresh, she said the first thing that came into her head. 'That you have interesting tastes.'

'Really? Do you?' he drawled nonchalantly.

'Yes, I believe so.'

'What about the pictures?' He nodded towards the impressive artwork.

So he had watched her studying those as well. 'I like them.'

His gaze narrowed. 'Do you know who painted them?'

'Yes.'

'How do you know?'

She raised her chin, trying to give an air of authority and calm. 'Though these are clearly originals, and I can only afford prints, Jonathan Cass and Marco Abruzzi are two of my favourite artists.'

He raised a dark, level brow. 'My, my, we *do* seem to have a lot in common. Wouldn't you say so?'

Clenching her teeth at the blatant mockery, she said nothing.

'So I take it you have the same pictures hanging in your living room?'

Aware that he thought she was making the whole thing up to curry favour, she answered briefly, 'No.'

'Ah, now you disappoint me. Do you actually have any by either of those artists?'

'I have two of Cass's and—'

'Which two?'

'*Snowfall* and *Winter Journey.*'

'Any of Abruzzi's?'

'Three,' she replied quickly.

'And they are?'

'*Olive Groves, Sunset* and *Fields of Sunflowers,*' she said, listing her three favorites.

'Do they all hang in the same room?'

'No…I would never have had the nerve to hang them together.'

'What do you think of the result?'

She wanted to say she hated it but, unable to frame the lie, she admitted, 'It shouldn't work, but somehow it does.'

'I'm pleased you think so,' he told her sardonically. 'Well, now we've established that when it comes to books and paintings we're practically soulmates, suppose you sit down and we'll see how you measure up on the business side.'

But she had had enough. If Zane Lorenson had realized who she was, he couldn't have been more unkind and derisive.

'Thank you,' she said stiffly, 'but I've decided I don't want the position after all, so there's no point in staying for the interview.'

Appearing totally unruffled, he asked, 'Why have you changed your mind?'

She had nothing to lose by speaking the truth. Lifting her chin and bravely meeting those green eyes, she told him, 'I don't like the way you're making fun of me. It's not business-like and—'

'You can't bear to be teased?'

'I can't see the necessity for it.'

'As a matter of fact, how a person reacts to being teased tells me quite a lot about his or her character. Now sit down.'

Though he spoke quietly, his voice cracked like a whip and, against all her inclinations, she found herself obeying a will stronger than her own.

CHAPTER TWO

As GAIL sank into the nearest armchair, her heart hammering against her ribs so loudly she felt sure it must be audible, he commented, 'That's better.'

Then, with exaggerated politeness, 'How do you like your coffee, Miss North?'

Her empty stomach was churning and, about to say she didn't want any coffee, she thought better of it and answered, 'A little cream, no sugar, thank you.'

'Exactly how I like mine,' he observed. Adding provokingly, 'Now, isn't that strange?'

Refusing to rise to the bait, she put her bag on the floor and sat in silence while he filled two cups with the dark fragrant liquid and added a dash of cream to each of them.

Passing her a cup, he sat down opposite and looked at her with a gleam in his eye that showed he enjoyed being master of the situation.

Watching her bite her lip, he queried, 'Do I take it you're vexed because of a little gentle teasing?'

Without answering, she looked at him stonily.

'OK.' He sat back with a hint of a smile on his lips. 'Let's keep this strictly business—where are you from?'

Still riled, she answered quickly. 'I was born in the north-east—'

The moment the words were out, she could have bitten her tongue. She shouldn't have told him that. Rona had always teased her unmercilessly about her Geordie accent and it was the one thing that he might possibly remember.

She risked a quick glance at him and the little flare of satisfaction in those handsome eyes made her heart sink.

Had he guessed her identity?

No, surely not. It must be because he had managed to provoke her into speech.

His expression bland now, he asked, 'Whereabouts in the north-east?'

'Tyneside,' she answered reluctantly, certain he was still mocking her.

When he nodded, clearly absorbing the information, Gail looked up at him and cautiously studied his handsome profile. She had forgotten just how devastatingly attractive his white smile was, and her heart lurched crazily.

Not that she was still attracted to him, she told herself hastily. It was just remembering the past that had affected her so strongly.

While she tried to steady herself, she made a pretence of sipping her coffee.

She was hoping that he had let the subject drop when he asked casually, 'How long did you live in the north?'

'We left when I was twelve.'

'Why?'

She paused, worried about how much information to reveal but replied honestly. 'My father died when I was ten, and two years later my mother remarried.'

Everything she had told him so far was the exact truth, but if he wanted to delve any further into her family background, rather than admit that her stepfather had been American and they had moved to the States, she would have to resort to lies.

However, to her relief, he changed tack by saying, 'So fill

me in on your personal details—full name, age, where you live, previous work experience…'

'It's all in my CV.'

He leaned back and crossed his ankles, perfectly at ease. 'I dare say it is, Miss North. But I'd prefer to hear it from your own lips…'

It was so in keeping with his attitude that she should have expected it.

'You can start by telling me your Christian name.'

'Gail.'

'Short for Abigail?'

'Yes.' She had been praying that he would take the name at face value and not make the connection.

Her parents had always called her Abbey, but after pointing out that in books Abigail was usually a servant's name, her stepsister Rona had used her full name, apparently in an unkind attempt to belittle her.

It was one of the reasons that, when she and her mother had returned to England, she had started to call herself Gail.

'A nice old-fashioned name,' Zane Lorenson commented after a moment. 'So how do you come to be called Abigail?'

'It was my maternal grandmother's name.'

'Would you believe me if I told you *my* maternal grandmother was named Abigail?'

'No, I wouldn't,' she said shortly.

He threw back his head and laughed. 'Well, at least you're honest. But, in this case, mistaken. It happens to be the truth.'

Her mouth went dry as he added, his tone reflective, 'It's quite an unusual name these days. You don't meet many Abigails.' His gaze held hers as if suggesting there was more meaning to his words.

So he had known who she was all along, and that was why he'd treated her the way he had.

If it had been at all possible she would have made a run for it, but her old fear of him was back in force and she was frozen into immobility, unable to either move or speak.

Quite a few seconds had passed before she appreciated that his lean, tanned face showed no sign of the anger or hostility she would have expected had he known who she was. She was being ridiculous, and she knew it. She had to keep calm.

His expression held a kind of studied patience as he waited for an answer to a question she hadn't even heard.

'I—I'm sorry,' she stammered.

'I asked how old you were.'

'Twenty…' she paused '…six.' It was her first white lie and the words almost stuck in her throat as she pretended to be older than she was. She had to make sure he hadn't made the connection.

'Which school did you go to?'

'Langton Chase.' She had gone to the well-known all girls school for just a year after she and her mother had returned to England.

He placed it immediately. 'So you lived in Sussex?'

'Yes.'

'With your parents?'

Though after the separation there had only been her mother, she answered, 'Yes.'

'Do your parents still live there?'

She shook her head. 'They're both dead now.'

'Were you very close?'

'I was to my mother.'

'Any brothers or sisters?'

Family relationships were a minefield, and she answered briefly, 'No.'

He ran long, lean fingers over his smooth jaw before moving on to ask, 'How old were you when you left school?'

With a sigh of relief at the change of subject, she told him, 'Eighteen.'

'Then what?'

'I spent a year at St Helen's Business College before getting a job at Randalls.'

'And there you were…' he picked up her CV '…PA to David Randall.'

She nodded, then, all at once foreseeing a problem that Paul hadn't taken into account, she added hastily, 'After Mr Randall had a heart attack and retired, the company was closed down.'

Zane Lorenson's clear, long-lashed eyes pinned her. 'The financial news indicated that it had been bought by The Manton Group.'

Her heart sank but somehow she managed steadily, 'Yes, it was. They paid off the workers and closed it down as soon as it was legally theirs.'

'What do you think of Paul Manton?'

'W-what?' she stammered.

'I asked what you thought of Paul Manton. Presumably he did the negotiating and wielded the axe. Or was it someone else?'

'A Mr Desmond,' she said, seizing on the suggestion.

Mark Desmond, Paul's second in command, a bluff, hearty man she had disliked on sight, had come in with Paul a couple of times.

'I'm surprised. Manton usually enjoys doing his own dirty work… Tell me, what did you think of the decision to close Randalls down?'

'I thought it was totally wrong.' For perhaps the first time her tone held real conviction. 'It wasn't what Mr Randall had wanted or expected.'

He raised a brow, questioning her frankness. 'He couldn't have known what kind of men he was dealing with, otherwise he *would* have expected it.'

Then, with another swift change of subject, 'Where do you live?'

'In Kensington.'

'Which part of Kensington?' he pressed.

'Just off the West Brackensfield Road,' she answered reluctantly.

She had hoped he would leave it at that, but he asked, 'Whereabouts exactly?'

'Delafield House, Rolchester Square. I share a flat,' she went on, rambling a bit because she was nervous.

'Does that mean you have a live-in lover?'

She shook her head. 'No. It means I share with another girl.'

'Have you any ties or commitments at home?'

She shook her head.

'No steady boyfriend?'

She stuck as close to the truth as she could. 'I'm not seeing anyone just at the moment.'

Studying her heart-shaped face, with its small straight nose, beautiful almond eyes and dark winged brows, its flawless skin and pure bone-structure, he commented, 'That surprises me.' Then, drily, 'Or have you heard that I prefer my PA to be a free agent?'

Determined to avoid direct lies wherever possible, she said, 'I split up with Jason, my previous boyfriend, some six months ago.'

'And there's been no one since then?'

Forced into a direct lie, she surreptitiously crossed her fingers and said, 'No.'

'So you're still broken-hearted?' her tormentor asked, the old hateful mockery back.

'Are such personal questions really necessary?' she demanded, losing her cool.

'Oh, absolutely,' he assured her, his voice flippant. Then,

smiling a little at her indignation, 'You see I don't want to take on a lovelorn PA whose mind isn't on her work.'

'I am *not* lovelorn,' she informed him raggedly.

'Does that mean you've got over it? Or you didn't love him in the first place?'

The unholy gleam in his eyes telling her that this was just another attempt to bait her, she bit back the angry words, took a deep breath and repeated more calmly, 'I am *not* lovelorn.'

With an ironic smile, he saluted that show of anger management before asking, 'Do you have any objections to travelling?'

On firmer ground now, she replied, 'None at all.'

'Done much?'

'Not as much as I would have liked. Europe mainly…' After her mother's untimely death she had taken holidays with Joanne, one of the secretaries from Randalls.

'Ever been to the States?'

She should have seen that coming. Once again she crossed her fingers and lied. 'No.'

His cool green eyes studied her face and lingered there, and she had the strangest feeling that he knew perfectly well that she hadn't spoken the truth.

Unable to meet that probing gaze, she was forced to look away.

There was a long thoughtful pause, then he said, 'Tell me, do you usually wear glasses?'

Ambushed by the unexpected question, she hesitated fractionally before saying as steadily as possible, 'Why, yes.'

'Strange. When I asked Mrs Rogers to describe you, she failed to mention them.'

Leaning over, he lifted the glasses from Gail's nose and squinted through them, before asking, 'Why do you wear them?'

'Why?'

'Yes, why? As far as I can see, these are merely low-strength reading glasses.'

Feeling her colour rise, she said nothing.

He handed them back to her. 'So you don't wear glasses as a rule. You put them on especially for this interview.'

Both were statements rather than questions, but her failure to dispute either was answer enough.

'Why did you feel that was necessary?'

Cursing the impulse that had made her put them on, she stammered, 'Well I—I thought they would make me look more…efficient, more competent…'

His green eyes glinted. 'That reason hardly inspires confidence. It strongly suggests that you aren't at all sure of yourself or your capabilities.'

'I'm quite sure I'm capable of doing the job.'

'Possibly you are, but lying to me is hardly the way to get it.'

So she had failed.

All she could feel for a moment or two was a sense of relief that she wouldn't have to go through with something she had dreaded.

Hard on the heels of that relief came a leaden feeling of failure as she realized just how angry and disappointed Paul would be.

Then both those feelings were swamped by the urgent necessity to leave, to get away from Zane Lorenson's clear-eyed scrutiny, his condemnation.

Gathering up her bag, she thrust the glasses clumsily into it and jumped to her feet, babbling, 'I'm sorry to have wasted your time…'

He rose too and took a step towards her. At five feet six inches she was fairly tall for a woman, but at well over six feet he seemed to tower over her. 'Don't rush off.'

Ignoring the quietly spoken order, she was about to head for the door when his lean fingers closed lightly round her wrist and kept her where she was. 'I said don't rush off.'

He had said that same thing to her once before and she shuddered as, his touch burning into her like a brand, she made an effort to pull free.

It was to no avail and, panic-stricken, recalling that past encounter and desperate to escape, she tried harder. 'Please let me go.'

Ignoring her plea, he put his free hand on her shoulder and pressed her back into the chair. Then, releasing her wrist, he stood over her.

Her voice sounding high and frightened even to her own ears, she objected, 'You've no right to keep me here against my will.'

Clicking his tongue, he told her severely, 'Now you're being melodramatic.'

His words were like a dash of cold water and, realizing the justice of his remark, she took a deep steadying breath and apologized shamefacedly. 'I'm sorry. I really don't know what's got into me.'

'I dare say the prospect of being interviewed made you nervous,' he suggested with smooth mockery. Now, if you're still interested in the job, there are one or two things you ought to know…

'I expect my PA to be available for twenty-four hours a day if I think it's necessary. That's why I asked if you have any ties at home.

'More importantly, I always give my PA my complete trust and in return I expect discretion and one hundred per cent loyalty…'

His words made Gail feel hollow inside.

'Because of the occasional long hours, I'm flexible with

regard to the length and the number of holidays my PA takes, and the salary is generous…'

He quoted a figure that made Gail blink and she found herself thinking, no wonder his previous PA had been reluctant to leave.

'Oh, just one more thing. When we're away from the office I like a friendly, informal working atmosphere with the use of first names.

'Now, if you want it, the job is yours.'

She didn't. But the thought of Paul's anger prevented her from saying so. If there was still a chance, he would want her to grab it with both hands.

And, after the way Zane Lorenson had treated her, did she really care if he came a cropper? Wouldn't she be justified in cheering if he *could* be brought to his knees?

Yes, she would.

But the truth was that she didn't want to play any part in it. Didn't want to have to work closely with a man who had turned her whole life upside down once before, and who, she was forced to admit, might well have the power to do so again.

She had never met anyone else who had such an overwhelming effect on her. Just being with him was traumatic, turning the cool, competent woman she had become into a mass of nerves and making her feel like a gauche, insecure seventeen-year-old again.

If she didn't take the job, she knew Paul might never forgive her. But it was more than that—when it came to Zane Lorenson, Gail couldn't say no.

'Well?' There was the merest hint of impatience in Zane's voice.

Still she hesitated. If she said no, she would be free and Paul need never know that she had had the chance and turned it down.

Sorely tempted, she battled with her conscience. Her conscience won.

There was no way she could deceive the man she loved and was going to marry. It would be like living a lie…

Looking up and meeting Zane Lorenson's green eyes was like walking into a plate glass window.

She was still mentally reeling when he said silkily, 'You seem to be having a great deal of difficulty deciding.'

'Yes,' she stammered. 'Yes, I want it.'

She saw what appeared to be a look of almost savage relief and satisfaction cross his face.

It was gone instantly and she knew she must have been mistaken. He wouldn't care one way or the other whether or not she took the job. If she didn't take it, no doubt the next girl he interviewed would.

'Very well,' he said, his tone businesslike, 'it's yours for a three month trial period. I'll let my secretary know what's happening and get her to deal with all the details.

'I understand from Mrs Rogers that you're free to start at once?'

She nodded, though in truth she didn't want to start at all. The second the words, '*Yes, I want it,*' had been spoken she had regretted them.

'How did you get here?'

Momentarily thrown, she echoed, 'Get here?'

'Did you come by bus? Tube?'

After a brief hesitation, she answered, 'Taxi.'

'You have a current passport?'

She frowned, unsure where this conversation was heading. 'Yes.'

'Good. How long will it take you to pack a bag?'

'P-pack a bag? You mean to travel?'

'My, but you're quick,' he said with a hint of sarcasm.

She flushed. 'I'm sorry. It's just a bit sudden.'

Though Paul had warned her, *'Lorenson has a massive office complex in Manhattan and he likes his Personal Assistant to be free and unencumbered, to be available to travel to his New York offices with him at the drop of a hat,'* she hadn't expected to be going quite this soon.

'So how long?'

'Fifteen minutes.'

'Right. Let's get on our way. My private jet's waiting at the airport.' A hand beneath her elbow, he hurried her to the door.

Wits scattered by his touch, and feeling as though she had been caught up and swept along by a tidal wave, Gail found herself escorted to the lift.

As it carried them swiftly downwards, he said, 'I need to discuss something with my secretary, so perhaps you can get a taxi home to pick up your passport and luggage, then go on to meet me at the airport?'

'Of course.' She could always ask the driver to wait while she slipped inside for some money.

And this way, she thought with relief, she would have a breathing space, time to talk to Paul and let him know the score.

If she told him how Zane Lorenson had treated her, he might be concerned enough to forbid her to take the job…

She was warming herself with that small flicker of hope when—as though her companion knew exactly what was in her mind and was determined to thwart her—he said, 'On second thoughts, I'll only be with Claire for a short time so I might as well take you.'

Apart from needing to speak to Paul, she didn't like the idea of Zane Lorenson going anywhere near her flat. His knowing her address was one thing, his actually ending up on her doorstep another.

Just the thought made her feel vulnerable, exposed.

Biting back the panic, she said as levelly as possible, 'There's really no need for you to go to all that trouble. I can easily—'

'It isn't any trouble,' he told her crisply as the lift doors slid to behind them and they made their way down the corridor, 'and it makes more sense for us to go together.'

'Oh, but—'

'If you took a taxi to the airport you might have some difficulty finding me, so it'll save time in the long run.'

Knowing she couldn't keep arguing, she relapsed into silence, her teeth biting into her lower lip.

'Something wrong?' he queried, giving her a sidelong glance.

Damn the man, he never missed a thing. 'No, nothing,' she assured him.

'Quite sure? We don't want to start our relationship with any undisclosed issues or problems. I know it's the friction in the oyster that makes the pearl, but now you're my PA I'd like there to be harmony, complete trust and confidence between us.'

She was saved from having to answer by the office door opening and Mrs Bancroft appearing, a sheaf of papers in her hand.

'Ah, Claire, before we start for the airport, I need a minute or two of your time.'

'Of course, Mr Lorenson.' Turning on her heel, she led the way back inside.

Gail found herself shepherded into the office and given a seat.

Her thoughts busy, she paid scant attention while, quickly and precisely, Zane Lorenson issued his orders, ending, 'I may be gone for a couple of weeks, but I intend to remain incommunicado.

'If anything really urgent crops up that Dave can't handle, you know how to get hold of me. Otherwise, I don't want to be disturbed while I'm away.'

'I understand, Mr Lorenson.'

'Good. Then we'll be off. Perhaps you'll ask John to bring the car round?'

'Certainly, Mr Lorenson.' She lifted the phone. 'Shall I ask him to pick up your luggage?'

'It's already in the boot, thanks.' Turning to Gail, he queried, 'Ready to go, Miss North?'

The brisk question scattering Gail's thoughts like a gunshot scattered starlings, she got to her feet.

They went down in the lift without a word being spoken, but she was uncomfortably aware that he never took his eyes off her face.

As, his hand at her waist, they made their way across the foyer, the pretty blonde behind the reception desk smiled brightly and called an eager, 'Good morning, Mr Lorenson.'

'Morning, Miss Johnson,' he responded pleasantly. 'Settling in all right?'

'Very well, thank you, Mr Lorenson.' She gave him another sparkling smile and shot Gail a glance that was frankly envious.

Judging by the way this attractive girl was practically drooling over him, Gail could quite believe he had no trouble getting a woman to warm his bed whenever he wanted one.

Outside the impressive entrance a stylish black limousine was just drawing up. A moment later the uniformed chauffeur had jumped out and was standing by to open the door.

As they approached, he said, 'Good morning, Mr Lorenson,' with a respectful salute.

'Morning, John… On the way to the airport, will you stop at Delafield House, Rolchester Square? It's just off the West Brackensfield Road.'

'Certainly, sir.'

'How's the wife keeping?'

'Very well, considering, thank you, sir. The twins are due any day now.'

'Know what they're going to be?'

As Gail got into the luxurious car, she heard the middle-aged chauffeur answer proudly, 'A boy and a girl, sir.'

'Lucky man. When they arrive, I dare say your wife will be only too glad of some help, so take a couple of weeks paid leave. I'll be away, so you won't be needed here.'

'Why, thank you, sir,' the chauffeur exclaimed gladly. 'Jenny will be grateful. She's been wondering how she'd cope. But I told her, there's no need to worry, Mr Lorenson won't see us in a mess…'

Gail frowned. Though as far as *she* was concerned he'd been anything but easy to deal with, his consideration for his chauffeur didn't match the cold, uncaring image Paul had painted.

The thought of Paul made her wonder how she was going to manage to phone him. If Zane Lorenson stayed in the car while she went in to pack, it wouldn't be a problem. But if he decided to come in…

'You're looking worried,' he observed gravely, sliding in beside her and reaching over to fasten her seat belt. 'Something wrong?'

Feeling flustered by his nearness, the firm thigh pressing against hers, she moved away as inconspicuously as possible and said jerkily, 'No. No, nothing at all.'

The ironic glance he gave her confirmed that he had noticed her instinctive reaction to his closeness, but he merely observed, 'I thought you might have changed your mind about working for me.'

She longed to say that she had, but dared not until she had talked to Paul and got his blessing.

Instead she answered with what conviction she could muster, 'No, of course not, Mr Lorenson.'

'As I said, when we're away from the office I like a friendly, informal atmosphere, so make it Zane, and I'll call you Abigail.'

'I prefer Gail,' she said quickly.

'Then Gail it is.'

Very conscious of the fact that he was studying her profile, and struggling to keep her composure, she turned to look at him, remarking steadily, 'Yours is an unusual name.'

His white teeth gleamed in a smile before he told her wryly, 'I used to curse my father—who had a regrettable taste for Westerns and read a lot of stories by Zane Grey—until I discovered that my mother would have called me Tarquin.'

In spite of herself, Gail smiled. 'Yes, I see what you mean.'

His eyes on her face, he said softly, 'You're quite beautiful when you smile.'

If it had been his intention to destroy her hard won composure, he succeeded. Completely thrown by both by his words and his close scrutiny, she found herself blushing hotly.

A moment later she heard his quiet, satisfied chuckle, before he said with mock repentance, 'Dear me, now I've embarrassed you. I'm afraid I hadn't realized that some women are still capable of being embarrassed by a compliment.'

Gail sat as if turned to stone as he added caustically, 'Or anything else for that matter. Most of the females I've met, even as young as sixteen or seventeen, are able to throw themselves at a man without so much as a blush…'

Even as young as sixteen or seventeen… Oh, dear God, why had he said that unless he *knew?*

As she waited in an agony of fear and humiliation for the axe to fall, he went on, 'It's quite refreshing to meet a woman in her twenties who obviously doesn't belong in that category.'

So he *didn't* know. She released the breath she had been unconsciously holding. It was her own sense of guilt and shame that had turned a general reference into a specific incident.

Too wrung out to make any further attempt at conversation and wishing herself anywhere but where she was, she stared blindly ahead and made an effort to at least *appear* relaxed.

But while she remained taut as a drawn bow string she was well aware that her companion—who was leaning back, his long legs stretched negligently, his feet crossed neatly at the ankles—was completely at ease.

Nothing more was said until they turned into Rolchester Square and drew up outside the modern block of flats.

When the chauffeur opened the car door, as nonchalantly as possible, Gail told the man beside her, 'I'll be as quick as I can,' and hastily scrambled out.

She thought for a split second that she had succeeded in leaving him behind, but Zane followed on her heels, saying coolly, 'If you can rustle up a cup of coffee, I could certainly use one.'

'Of course,' she agreed hollowly.

It would be no use attempting to phone Paul now. The internal walls of the flat were paper-thin. Even if she spoke quietly, Zane was bound to realize she was talking to someone.

She could use her mobile to send a text, of course. But if Paul was busy he might not bother to pick up a text message until lunch time, and that would be far too late.

A second or two's thought convinced her that it would be better to wait until she reached the airport. Then she could slip into the Ladies' and phone him from there.

If he was willing to let her back out, she could tell Zane that she had had second thoughts and get a taxi home.

Feeling a shade happier, she fished in her bag for the key and let them both into her ground floor flat which, though small, was as pleasant as the two girls could make it.

Dropping her bag on the coffee table and indicating one of the linen-covered armchairs, she asked, 'Won't you sit down?'

But, ignoring the polite invitation, Zane followed her through to the tiny kitchen and leaned idly against one of the work surfaces while she put the kettle on and spooned coffee into the cafetière.

Feeling all thumbs because he was watching her, she said, 'I'm afraid we've only got milk. My flatmate's trying to lose weight and she refused to put cream on the shopping list.'

'Don't worry, I'm quite happy with it black.'

Seeing her get out, and fill, a single cup, he queried, 'Aren't you going to join me?'

Anxious to bring an end to this nerve-racking situation, she shook her head. 'I need to write a note for my flatmate before I start packing.'

If her appeal to Paul was successful, she could always tear the note up when she got back. If it wasn't—and that didn't bear thinking about—Lynne would need to know what was happening.

CHAPTER THREE

FINDING a pen and a piece of paper, Gail briefly explained the situation, adding that there was a possibility that she might be in the States for a week or two.

Then having propped the note against the kettle where her flatmate was sure to find it, she turned to go through to her bedroom.

'Don't bother to pack a flight bag,' Zane told her. 'There'll be everything you may need on the plane. But do remember to bring your passport,' he added as he took his coffee and returned to the living room.

She lifted her case from the top of the wardrobe and, hardly caring what she put in—as, hopefully, she wouldn't be needing any of it—packed it. Then, having zipped it up, she searched in the chest of drawers for her passport.

When she returned to the living room, her case in one hand, her passport in the other, Zane rose to his feet with a wholly masculine grace and said approvingly, 'You've been quick... Here, let me take care of those.'

He relieved her of the case and, before she could think of arguing, he'd taken the passport and slipped it into his pocket.

'Have you packed a swimsuit?'

'A swimsuit?' she echoed blankly.

Though a number of hotels boasted a swimming pool these days, she wouldn't have given it a thought even if she *had* intended to go through with the trip.

He shrugged dismissively. 'I can see you haven't. Never mind. I'm sure we'll be able to sort out the problem when the time comes. Now, all set?'

Picking up her shoulder bag, she nodded.

'Then let's go.' He shepherded her to the door.

During the drive to the airport he seemed occupied with his thoughts. Gail, who couldn't wait to get there, sat staring into space, silently repeating, *Please let Paul understand*...like a mantra.

Though they had a good run through, it seemed an age before they reached the busy airport and made their way to a special VIP parking area.

It was only as they drew up that Gail realized she had still forgotten to pick up her notecase.

As the chauffeur jumped out to open the car door, a young, smartly dressed man who had obviously been awaiting their arrival hurried over.

'Good morning, Mr Lorenson.'

'Morning, Derek. How are things?'

'Fine, thank you, sir. If you'd like to come through, your luggage will all be taken care of.'

Rather than striding ahead and leaving her to follow at his heels, as Paul was apt to do, Zane picked up his briefcase and, putting a hand at her waist, kept her by his side as they made their way into the airport buildings.

While he quickly dealt with the checks and procedures, Gail remained sunk in thought, doing her best to plan ahead.

When the formalities were over, instead of handing her back her passport, he put it in his briefcase with the rest of the documents.

Watching it disappear with a sinking heart, she realized that things had gone a lot further than she had intended and she might have to abandon both her passport and her luggage and make a run for it…

But first she had to speak to Paul.

'If you don't mind,' she said hurriedly, 'I just need to pay a visit to the Ladies.'

He put a restraining hand on her arm. 'We're running a little late—there's a perfectly good bathroom on the plane.'

'Oh, but I—'

'As we already have a take-off slot,' he added with a commanding edge to his voice, 'we shall be boarding immediately.'

Before she could catch her breath, she found herself escorted outside and across the tarmac to a sleek executive jet which was standing gleaming in the late morning sunshine.

The moment they had been welcomed aboard by a middle-aged, cheerful-faced steward, Zane remarked, 'Miss North is desperate to wash her hands, so will you show her where the bathroom is, please, Jarvis?'

'Certainly, sir. If you'll follow me, Miss North.'

Turning to Gail, Zane said, 'While you're gone I'll have a quick word with Captain Giardino and then we'll be about ready for take-off.'

Though his face was straight, she knew by the gleam in his eye that he not only knew how embarrassed she felt, but was amused by her discomfort.

Biting her lip and keeping a tight hold on both her temper and her bag, she followed the steward's white-coated figure to the rear of the plane, where she was shown into a small but luxurious bathroom.

She murmured her thanks and, the moment the door was shut and the bolt pushed firmly into place, unzipped her bag and felt for her mobile.

If she was quick enough there was still a chance she could talk to Paul and get off the plane before the luggage arrived and the main door was closed.

To start with, her fumbling fingers failed to locate it and, cursing the fact that everything was jumbled together in the bottom, she made a more thorough search.

The seconds were ticking away rapidly and when she still couldn't find it, frantic now, she tipped the entire contents of her bag into the sink and scrabbled through them.

It was a moment before she could really believe what her eyes were confirming. It wasn't there.

But she couldn't possibly have lost it. She had taken it off charge and put it in her bag that morning while Paul had stood and waited for her and she hadn't opened her bag since, apart from taking out and putting back the glasses.

Still, the hideous fact remained that *it wasn't there* and the only time the bag had been out of her sight was when she had left it in the living room while she'd gone to pack.

Suppose Zane had taken it?

Oh, don't be a fool, she told herself crossly. Why on earth should he take my phone?

Unless he had known precisely what she had in mind.

The thought momentarily sent her brain reeling.

But he couldn't possibly have known. She was being utterly ridiculous. If he'd had any idea of her link with Paul he would never have offered her the job in the first place.

Common sense having restored the balance, her mind went back to the more pressing problem of what she was to do now.

There were two options. She could throw everything away by telling Zane she didn't want the job after all and insist on leaving the plane. Or she could go through with this trip to the States and see how things worked out.

If she chose the former without consulting him, there was a

good chance that Paul, whom she knew bore grudges, might never forgive her. If she chose the latter, she would have to find some way of armouring herself against Zane Lorenson…

A tap at the door made her practically jump out of her skin.

'I'm sorry to disturb you, Miss North,' the steward's voice murmured discreetly, 'but Mr Lorenson asked me to let you know that any minute now we'll be starting to taxi in preparation for take-off.'

With a jolt, Gail faced the fact that she had left it too late. She no longer had a choice.

Somehow she found her voice and answered, 'Please tell him I'll be there in just a moment.'

Having transferred her belongings from the sink back into her bag, Gail hurried after the steward, much too harassed to be more than vaguely aware of her sumptuous surroundings.

They were already taxiing towards the runway, any minute now they would be airborne, and Paul didn't even know she'd got the job, let alone that she would soon be on her way to the States.

It was scant consolation when her common sense reminded her that if he didn't hear anything, he would no doubt get in touch with Lynne and find out what was happening.

When she reached the forward cabin, Zane was leaning against the bulkhead, waiting for her. He'd discarded his jacket and his crisp, white shirt made him look a little more relaxed, but just as ruthless.

'No problems, I trust?' he asked lazily.

'No, none at all,' she answered as levelly as possible and wondered what lay behind the question.

But she mustn't start attributing ulterior motives to everything he said, she told herself firmly, otherwise she would get paranoid.

Seemingly unaware of her worries, he helped her off with

her jacket, settled her into a window seat and fastened her belt before taking his place beside her.

Feeling trapped, panicky, she very much regretted getting on the plane. But it was too late for regrets, so somehow she would have to make the best of it. The thought failed to cheer her.

While they waited at the top of the runway, as though picking up on her feelings, Zane turned his head to ask, 'Scared?'

When she was younger she had been afraid of flying but, after Rona had teased her mercilessly about it, she had learnt to overcome that fear. Or at least hide it.

Now, in order to explain her only too obvious agitation, she considered agreeing that she was scared but, realizing that he might tie it in with the past, she denied hurriedly, 'No.'

'That's funny. You give the impression you are.'

'I'm not at all scared.'

'Sure? If you are, I'll be more than happy to hold your hand.' He proffered a tanned, well-shaped hand with neatly trimmed nails.

Flinching, she insisted, 'Quite sure. I don't know why you think I might be.'

'Being scared is no disgrace. My previous PA was until she got used to being on a smaller plane.'

'Though I've always travelled on one of the big commercial jets, being on a smaller plane doesn't really bother me.' She tried to keep her voice level.

He smiled. 'Judging by your reaction, having me hold your hand would bother you a great deal more.'

Realizing he was deliberately teasing her, she clenched her teeth and stared resolutely out of the window while the plane began to taxi down the runway, gathering speed.

Their take-off was smooth and effortless and, after climbing steeply through a scattering of cotton wool clouds, they were soon at the right altitude.

When they levelled out, Zane unfastened both their seat belts and suggested, 'Would you like to come up front and meet the Captain?'

At her nod of acquiescence, he turned and led the way into the cockpit. There, while Gail stared in fascination at the banks of dials and instruments, he and the pilot briefly talked technicalities.

Then, with a smile, Zane made the introduction. 'Gail, this is Captain Giardino… Carlo, I'd like you to meet Miss North.'

She couldn't help but notice—and wonder why—he'd simply given her name without mentioning that she was his new PA.

Captain Giardino was a nice-looking, middle-aged man with dark, greying hair and light hazel eyes. Returning her smile, he said pleasantly, 'It's nice to meet you, Miss North.'

For all his Italian name he spoke perfect English with only the slightest of accents.

Then, showing he'd noticed her interest in the instrument panel, he went on, 'Believe me, it's not half as complicated as it looks. These days planes like this practically fly themselves.'

Gravely, Zane said, 'I'm not at all sure you should mention that. Though she won't admit it, Gail is a bit nervous of flying, so I'm sure she'd prefer an experienced pilot to be in charge.'

Giving Gail a sympathetic grin, the Captain said chivalrously, 'In that case, I promise I'll stay on the job.'

After the two men had had a short discussion about flying conditions, Zane and Gail returned to the forward cabin. As they reached it, he queried, 'What time did you have breakfast this morning?'

Much too worked up to eat, she had swallowed a cup of coffee at about six-thirty.

When she failed to answer, he suggested, 'Or maybe you didn't have any?'

'No, I didn't.'

'You couldn't eat because you were anxious about the interview?'

She nodded.

He disappeared into the galley, to return almost immediately. 'I've asked Jarvis to serve the food as soon as it's ready, so in the meantime let's go and have a pre-lunch drink.'

She found herself escorted into the sumptuous lounge area and seated in one of the soft, natural leather armchairs.

Crossing to a small, well-stocked bar, Zane queried, 'What would you like? A gin and tonic, perhaps?'

'A soft drink of some kind, please.'

'That might be wise on an empty stomach.'

While he put crushed ice and fruit juices into the thick glass tumbler, she watched him covertly.

As he looked down, momentarily absorbed in what he was doing, his lips were slightly pursed and long dark lashes seemed to almost brush his hard cheeks.

He hadn't the kind of film star, slightly effeminate good looks that Paul had, but a tough masculine face, his profile clean-cut and handsome, with a straight nose and a strong jaw. A fascinating face that had, from the start, moved her and made her feel a strange ache inside.

When he reached for a glass her gaze dropped to his hands, which were lean and long-fingered and, as she knew to her cost, had a whipcord strength. She recalled how they had held her, how they had…

With a shiver she snapped off the thought and looked away. In her present predicament it wouldn't help to dwell on the past.

As he put a tall frosted glass into her hand his fingers brushed against hers and what felt like an electric shock tingled up her arm, making her almost spill the contents.

'Still nervous, I see.'

'Not at all,' she denied huskily. 'I just thought for a moment that I was going to drop it.'

Though it was obvious he didn't believe her, he made no further comment.

Pulling herself together, she took a sip. It was cool and fresh and tangy, and she nodded her approval. 'It's very nice, thank you.'

Smiling a little mockingly at her schoolgirl politeness, he picked up his own glass and sat down opposite her.

As she sipped, starting to feel the tension, she tried to think of something to say.

Without success.

Then a soft tap heralded the steward, who wheeled in a loaded trolley, then quickly and deftly transferred everything to a small dining table by one of the windows and set a couple of chairs in place. 'Will that be all, sir?'

'Yes, thank you, Jarvis. We'll help ourselves.'

When the man had gone, Zane rose to his feet, pulled out Gail's chair and seated her, before asking courteously, 'Would you prefer seafood or sandwiches?'

She swallowed. 'Seafood will be fine, thank you.'

He filled two plates with seafood and salad and placed one in front of her. 'Make a start on that; you must be ravenous.'

Anxiety lying like a lead weight in her stomach, she had never felt less like eating and, though it all looked delicious, she picked up her knife and fork with reluctance.

Having helped them both to a glass of Orvieto, he lifted his own in a toast. 'Here's to our future relationship. May it be a good and lasting one.'

As she took a sip of the dry white wine, she wondered why he hadn't said *working* relationship.

But that thought was lost as, apparently making an effort to put her at her ease, he set the conversational ball rolling by saying lightly, 'It's time we started to get to know one anther, so tell me about yourself.'

When, wondering what she could safely tell him, she hesitated, he prompted, 'For instance, what kind of music do you enjoy?'

She paused, trying to gather her thoughts. 'Mainly classical, some middle-of-the-road, some pop, some jazz...'

'What about opera?'

She nodded a little nervously, aware of their close proximity. 'Yes, I like opera.'

'Do you have a favourite composer?'

'Puccini.'

'A romantic, I see...'

Their discussion continued, more often than not their opinions and tastes corresponded and the few times they differed it was on minor issues.

He proved to be an interesting and entertaining companion, easy to talk to and with a ready turn of phrase and an unexpected sense of humour.

It all seemed so normal, so unthreatening, that she found herself starting to relax.

They had moved to the armchairs to drink their coffee when there was a tap and the steward came in to announce, 'If you've finished your lunch, sir, there's something Captain Giardino would like to check with you.'

'Thanks, Jarvis. You can clear away now.'

While the remains of lunch were whisked away, Zane emptied his coffee cup and, rising to his feet, said politely, 'If you'll excuse me, I'll go and see what Carlo wants.'

'Of course.'

'There's a selection of CDs you can look at or, if you'd prefer to read, plenty of books.'

'Thank you.' She watched his broad back as he walked away,

noting how his thick dark hair grew in a duck's tail in the nape of his neck.

It was one of the first things she had noticed about him all those years ago.

She had been living in her stepfather's downtown Seventh Avenue apartment then, and had been just about to leave her room one evening when she'd realized that Rona's latest boyfriend had arrived to collect her.

Disliking the kind of men her stepsister usually chose—men who thought it was fun to make smart alec remarks and pretend to flirt with her—she'd decided to wait until the pair had gone and, leaving the door slightly ajar, had peered through the crack.

He'd been sitting on the settee, his back to her. At first he'd seemed to be relaxed, at his ease, but then, as if he could sense her gaze, he'd turned his head. Although common sense had told her he couldn't see her, she had jerked back immediately.

After a moment or two she had taken another cautious peep. He had moved his position and this time she'd been rewarded by the sight of his clear-cut, handsome profile. A profile that had immediately bewitched her.

As though mesmerised, she had continued to watch until Rona had come in wearing a stunning scarlet evening gown and a white ermine stole, her blonde beauty as dazzling as the jewels her proud father had lavished on her.

The handsome young man rose to his feet. He was tall and broad-shouldered, she saw, and wearing immaculate evening dress.

Taking both Rona's hands, he told her, 'You look absolutely sensational.'

His voice was deep and attractive.

Well used to compliments, Rona appeared a little bored and, when he would have drawn her close and kissed her, she fended him off. 'Not now, darling, you'll ruin my make-up and we're none too early as it is.'

As he opened the door and held it, Gail saw him full face for the first time and when he smiled at something Rona had said, her heart lurched crazily.

The pair left then, while she looked after them with a sigh.

Most of Rona's boyfriends—the spoilt, decadent sons of prominent society couples—appeared bored and effete.

But this man was different. Though he could have only been about twenty-three or -four, he had a maturity, a power, that the others had lacked. Apart from his very masculine good looks, there was something real and vital about him, something charismatic that drew her like a magnet.

She discovered that his name was Zane Lorenson and over the next few weeks she lived for his visits, watching him covertly whenever she got the opportunity.

At first only her mother noticed her obsession. But then Rona caught on and, with that inherent streak of cruelty, started to make her life even more of a misery than she'd made it for the past five years.

Her scarlet lip curling, she taunted, 'So you've got the hots for him, have you? Go on, you might as well admit it. Your face gives you away.'

'I just think he's nice,' Gail muttered defensively.

'You just think he's nice?' Rona mimicked her Geordie accent, which became more pronounced when she was stressed. 'Then why don't you see what you can do to attract him?'

As Gail began to shake her head, Rona went on, 'I'll be finishing with him soon.'

'Finishing with him?'

'Yes. It's a great pity he's not wealthy. Not only is he generous, but he's a fantastic lover.' She sighed. 'I must say it's been great while it lasted, but I'm on the lookout for a seriously rich man.

'So, when I'm ready to give him the brush-off, would you like me to tell him that, as far as you're concerned, he's got it made?'

Looking horrified, Gail begged, 'Please, Rona, don't say anything…'

Rona laughed. 'Don't worry. Apart from the fact that you wouldn't know how to deal with a red-blooded man like that, timid little virgins aren't his style.

'If he needs consolation, glamorous blondes with model-girl figures are more up his street. He wouldn't look twice at a lank-haired, flat-chested, spotty schoolgirl…'

With Rona's derisive words ringing in her ears, Gail made up her mind to use the money she had been given for her seventeenth birthday to change her drab image.

She bought face-packs to clear her skin, had her straight dark hair turned into a frizz of long blonde curls and bought herself some make-up and a selection of pretty briefs and padded bras.

Only to find herself jeered at and made fun of even more by her stepsister.

Keeping a low profile, she did her best to ignore the cruel teasing in the hope that it would stop. But a few evenings later Rona walked into her room and, seizing her arm, almost dragged her into the living room.

To Zane Lorenson, who was standing there, Rona announced, 'This is my little sister, Abigail…Abigail is your secret admirer…'

Looking amused, he raised a dark brow.

'She fancies she's in love with you, and the hairdo, the make-up and the new padded bra are all for your benefit…'

Her face scarlet, Gail tried unsuccessfully to pull free.

'I'm sure she would happily give you her all. But, even with such an incentive, I'm afraid you'd soon be bored. She's a poor spineless creature. She'd never have the nerve to stand up to you…'

Looking anything but amused now, Zane ordered, 'Stop being bitchy, Rona, and let the child go.'

As soon as her stepsister's grip relaxed, Gail fled back to her room.

The feeling of shame and humiliation brought stinging tears and, for the first time since coming to live in New York, she gave way to them and cried.

Her only faint consolation was that Zane Lorenson had intervened on her behalf. Though it stung that he had referred to her as a child.

The unpleasant little scene had been overheard by her mother and stepfather, Martin, and caused the older pair to have yet another row.

This one was even more bitter than usual and Gail heard her mother threaten to leave him if he didn't stop Rona being so nasty.

In the days that followed, apparently on her father's orders, Rona left Gail severely alone and a couple of weeks passed without any further painful incidents.

Her stepfather went to 'have a drink' at his club most nights and her mother did voluntary work at their local church's Shelter for the Homeless. So on the evenings she knew Zane would be calling—though part of her ached to catch just a glimpse of him or hear his voice—Gail took good care to be out.

To have somewhere to go, she paid a subscription and joined in the Youth Leisure activities that took place in Greenwich Village. It was reasonably close to where they lived so most times, especially if it was fine, she walked there and back.

The theatre club were meeting that Friday to discuss their next production and, though Gail was far too shy to want a part, she was quite willing to lend a hand behind the scenes.

Earlier in the evening, before going their separate ways, her mother and her stepfather had fallen out yet again.

It seemed that Martin, who had turned out to be a petty dictator, had taken an unreasonable dislike to his wife's involvement with the Shelter and had ordered her not to go.

But this time she had dug her heels in and refused to let him rule her, and what had started as a minor disagreement had ended in a full scale row.

Upset by her stepfather's ranting and raving, and her mother's white, set face, Gail couldn't wait to get out of the apartment.

She was almost ready to leave when there was a perfunctory knock at her bedroom door and Rona came in, beautifully made-up and looking ravishing in a blue silk suit.

Handing Gail an envelope, she said shortly, 'When you go to the theatre club I want you to drop this in at Denver House, apartment 2B. You have to pass the end of Denver Street, so it's barely a block out of your way.'

Her mouth going dry, Gail stammered, 'B-but isn't that where…?'

'Zane lives? Yes, it is. I'd agreed to go to his place tonight but—'

'Well, if you're going there—'

'That's just the point; I'm not now. Something's cropped up and I've got other plans.'

Then, her aquamarine eyes impatient, 'Don't worry, you don't need to see him. Just push the envelope under the door.'

'Oh, but—'

'Denver House is an old place with just a janitor who lives in the basement. There's none of the tight security we have here. All you need to do is go on in and walk up.'

Far from happy, Gail asked, 'Why can't you just phone him?'

'A few minutes ago, while I was in my bedroom packing, I came across his Amex card and the key I gave him to this place.

They must have slipped out of his wallet last night when he was getting either dressed or undressed.

'Because of the way things are turning out, I've decided to keep the key. But I don't want him coming round here to collect his credit card—he's been a regular visitor and security know him, so they'd let him in even without a key—that's why I'm returning the card with a note to explain that I'm ill.'

'You don't look ill.'

Rona sighed. 'I'm not.'

'Then why lie about it?' Gail couldn't understand why she wouldn't want to see Zane.

'Because I'm flying out to spend a...shall I say *private* weekend on Johnny Chator's yacht.'

Appalled, Gail exclaimed, 'You don't mean...?'

'That's exactly what I mean,' Rona said with satisfaction, 'and I don't want Zane to find out. I imagine that if he knew I was two-timing him he could be quite formidable.

'One day he may well be rich himself, but I can't afford to wait. After some failed investments, Daddy's on the verge of bankruptcy, that's why he's started to drink so heavily.' Rona studied her immaculate nails.

'It's only a matter of time before the news becomes common knowledge, and I'd like a ring on my finger and a wealthy husband before that happens...'

Gail had known for some time that her stepfather was in difficulties and, though she had never liked him, she couldn't help but feel a certain sympathy for him.

'Now Johnny's back in circulation after his last trip to Reno,' Rona went on, 'and he may just be the answer to my prayers. It's rumoured that as well as a little fun and excitement, which I'm more than willing to provide, he's looking for wife number five. He likes his women young, and I'll soon be twenty-four, so there's no time to waste.'

Shocked, Gail protested, 'But he's old and ugly.'

'I agree he's not exactly an oil painting, and he's known to be a bit of a rake, but he's reputed to be one of the richest men in New York.

'Even if the marriage didn't last long, the sort of alimony he pays would set me up for life—it's known as marrying well and divorcing better—so, if all goes according to plan and he takes the bait this weekend, I'll give Zane the brush.'

Incensed on Zane's behalf, Gail began indignantly, 'I don't know how you can be so—'

Rona gave her a disdainful glance. 'Save the preaching and, whatever you do, don't forget to deliver that note.'

Glancing at her watch, she added smugly, 'I must fly. Johnny's sending a limo for me and I don't want to keep him waiting.' She hurried away.

Looking down at the envelope in her hand, Gail clenched her teeth. She hated the way Rona had talked about Zane, hated her willingness to deceive him.

But of course it was more than that that was making her feel hollow inside, she admitted silently. The last thing she wanted was to have to go anywhere near Zane Lorenson's apartment.

So what was she to do?

She could either put the envelope in the post or do nothing.

But if she did either of those, when Rona failed to turn up at his place this evening, he would no doubt come round here to see what was wrong.

And when he found no one in, then what?

Doubtless he would keep coming until he got some kind of answer.

Which would put Rona in a spot. And if her weekend away hadn't gone according to plan and she wanted to keep Zane a little longer…

Well, if everything blew up in her face she only had herself to blame, a little demon pointed out. Not only was she treating Zane shabbily, but she shouldn't have tried to make someone else do her dirty work.

So why not put her in a spot?

CHAPTER FOUR

No, GAIL thought, sending the little demon packing, she just couldn't do it. Though from the start her stepsister had been as unpleasant as possible, and she owed her nothing, two wrongs didn't make a right.

She would have to deliver the envelope. And getting some kind of explanation for Rona's failure to turn up would spare Zane's feelings.

At least for the time being.

Having pulled on a light jacket, Gail thrust the envelope into one of the big square pockets, picked up her shoulder-bag and, apprehension hanging over her like a dark cloud, took the lift down.

She had started to cross the lobby when one of the blue-uniformed security guards appeared and she recognized a familiar face that she hadn't seen for some months.

Gail had always liked Patrick O'Brian and pleasure at seeing him well and on his feet again made her, for a short time at least, forget her anxiety.

The tall, thick-set figure approached, beaming at her. 'Well, well, I almost didn't recognize you. You've gone and altered the colour of your hair as well as the style.'

'Yes, I... I felt like a change.'

'So how are you, Miss Abbey?'

'Very well, thank you, Patrick… It's nice to see you back. I heard you'd been badly injured in a road accident,' Gail said, concerned.

'That I was, Miss Abbey. They practically gave me up for dead at one time, but I pulled through and now I'm back at work and nearly as good as new…'

In spite of living in the States for over twenty years, he still had the traces of an Irish accent.

'I wasn't expecting to start until next week, but both Frank and Ira have flu, so I'm holding the fort by myself for a day or two. It looks like it might be a busy time. I was told there'd been a security scare a couple of days ago—an intruder was spotted inside the building.'

Gail gasped. 'An intruder? How did he get in without a key?'

'When one of the tenants let herself in, this man just walked in with her, cool as you like, saying he was visiting someone.

'Then only yesterday Mrs Williams reported an attempted break-in in broad daylight. So warn your folks to be on their guard.'

'Everyone's out tonight, but I'll tell them when they get back. Though I do hope there won't be any trouble when you're on your own.'

Patrick laughed. 'Don't worry, the cops will be on hand if I need any help.' He checked his watch. 'Well, I'd best get on. Don't forget now, if you see anyone knocking about that looks suspicious, let me know straight away.'

'I will.'

As Patrick walked away, the dark cloud descended once more as Gail remembered the task in hand.

It was a fine summery evening, the streets crowded with traffic and pedestrians. There was a touch of *joie de vivre* in the air—New York at its best—and any other time she would have thoroughly enjoyed the walk. But this time apprehension walked with her and she couldn't wait to get the dreaded errand over.

But she was just being silly, she scolded herself, it was no big deal. All she had to do was slip the envelope under the door and walk away. He would never know she had been anywhere near.

When she reached the old house on Denver Street, she climbed the stoop and—not without some trepidation—walked straight in, just as Rona had said she could.

Though it wasn't in the least luxurious, everywhere appeared to be clean and well cared for and as she climbed the stairs she noticed that the air was fresh and smelled faintly of pine.

On the second floor she located the apartment she was looking for and held her breath as she crept up to the door and, stooping, tried to slide the envelope beneath it.

But the door was a much better fit than she had anticipated and she was forced to make several attempts before she finally succeeded.

Breathing a ragged sigh of relief, she was just turning away when the door opened abruptly and Zane stood there, the envelope in his hand, his handsome face alert, questioning.

Momentarily rooted to the spot, she stood and stared at him.

At first he didn't recognise her and then, as realisation dawned, he smiled, intrigued as to her purpose. 'Well, well, well, look who's here. Do come in.'

'I—I can't stop, really, I'm—'

Ignoring her protest, he took her arm, his touch, and the masterful look on his face, making her insides turn to jelly. 'I'm sure you can spare just a minute or two to tell me what this is all about.'

'There's a note from Rona that will explain everything,' she said desperately.

'I'd much prefer to hear it from you,' he drawled lazily.

Before she could make any further protest, she found herself drawn into a small inner hallway and the door closed firmly behind her.

'Through here.' Zane indicated a door opposite that stood invitingly open.

Having steered her to a couch and waited while she sank on to it, he stood for a moment or two looking down at her.

Part of her mind registered that the living room was light and pleasant and that a table had been set for a romantic dinner for two, but all her attention was focused on him.

He was wearing well-cut trousers and a toning dark shirt open at the neck to expose the strong, tanned column of his throat. His thickly lashed eyes were brilliant and a stray lock of dark hair fell over his forehead.

His gaze was piercing and it set her on edge. 'So what's going on, exactly?'

Her heart racing, her wits scattered by his nearness and the powerful effect he had on her, she couldn't have said a word to save her life.

As, her beautiful grey eyes wide and defenceless, she stared up at him, he remarked, 'There's no need to look quite so scared.' His voice was softer, but still held that quiet authority that had her so worried. 'I'm not the big bad wolf, you know.'

When she still said nothing, he sat down opposite her. 'Suppose you start by telling me why you're here instead of Rona?'

When she had found her voice, Gail began, a shade unsteadily, 'I pass the end of your street on my way to the theatre club and Rona asked me to—'

'*Told* you to, if I know Rona. But do go on.'

'To push a note under your door—'

He frowned. 'Why a note?'

'Because she can't come tonight and—'

'I mean, why didn't she phone me?'

'She said you'd lost your Amex card—' recalling *exactly* what Rona had said, Gail felt her colour rising '—and she wanted you to have it back.'

His eyes alight with amusement, as if he knew precisely why she was blushing, he said, 'I see. So why can't she come?'

'She's…' The lie stuck in Gail's throat and she was forced to swallow. 'She's ill.'

'She was fine last night.'

Then, as though reading her mind and picking up her feeling of guilt that she was concealing the truth, he demanded, 'What's wrong with her?'

'I—I don't know.'

He frowned. 'Surely you've some idea?'

Growing even more uncomfortable, she stammered, 'Not really… I m-mean she didn't tell me.'

Those clear forest-green eyes pinned her and it was obvious that he knew she was lying.

Jerkily, she asked, 'Why don't you read the note? That's sure to say.'

He opened the envelope, put the credit card to one side and, unfolding the note, scanned it quickly.

Seeing a chance to escape while his attention was distracted, Gail rose to her feet.

She had taken only a couple of steps when he glanced up and, tossing the note on to the coffee table, said, 'I must say that sounds like a load of claptrap.'

Though he looked anything but concerned, she could tell that underneath he was angry and, every muscle tense, she was ready for flight, when he queried, 'Wouldn't you agree?'

Wanting only to get away, she said shortly, 'I've no idea what Rona's told you.'

'She says that she's picked up some kind of bug and is too ill to get out of bed. She just wants to be left alone until she feels better.'

'Oh…' Gail stumbled over what else to say.

'You said you didn't know what was wrong with her, but if she really is as ill as all that, you must have known.' Then he paused, letting the silence hang in the air. Gail swallowed nervously. Then he continued, 'Of course, if *being ill* is just an excuse, then you *wouldn't* know, although, as her messenger, I do think she might have briefed you better…'

When she remained silent, his face sardonic, he added, 'But she was expecting you to just leave the note and run, wasn't she?'

Ignoring the question, Gail started for the door on legs that shook.

'Come back and sit down.'

Though Zane spoke quietly, his voice cracked like a whip. But, at the end of her tether, she kept going.

He easily reached the door first. 'I said come back and sit down.'

Though scared half to death, she lifted her chin and looked him in the eye. 'I can't. I'll be late for the theatre club.'

'Too bad. Now, are you coming back or do I have to carry you?'

There was something about the way he spoke that made her know he meant it and, terrified that he would carry out his threat, she retraced her steps and sat down.

'That's better,' he murmured, making no attempt to hide his satisfaction.

Riled by the way he was enjoying riding roughshod over her, she gave him a mutinous glance.

'So you do have some spirit after all,' he observed mockingly. 'I was starting to think that you might be the poor spineless creature that Rona called you…'

Gritting her teeth, she said nothing.

Looming over her, tall and dark and dangerous, he said softly, 'Now, let's have the truth. *Is* Rona ill?'

'Why would she say she is if she isn't?'

He smiled grimly. 'An intriguing question, to which I'd like an answer.'

'I've no intention of answering any more questions. I'm going to be late for the club and I want to leave this minute.'

'You can leave when you've told me exactly what Rona's up to.'

'I don't know what you mean.' Gail felt her voice break as tears threatened.

'You know perfectly well what I mean. What is she up to that she doesn't want me to know about?'

'I've no idea.' She hoped he would believe her but, naturally honest, she found it almost impossible to sound convincing.

'You're not a very good liar.' He smiled wolfishly and watched her soft mouth tighten. 'So why not try telling me the truth?'

Knowing she had reached the end of the road and that she would have to get out of there fast, in desperation she decided to carry the war into the enemy camp.

Rising to her feet, she said as steadily as possible, 'I've no intention of telling you anything further. I'm leaving now and if you try to stop me I'll scream the place down.'

He raised a brow mockingly. 'I don't believe you have the courage to make a scene.'

'Try me.'

When she reached the outer door without interference, she knew she'd won.

A feeling of triumph flooding through her, she had started to turn the knob when she was seized from behind and swung round.

She drew a deep breath but, before she could carry out her threat, he pulled her roughly into his arms and his mouth covered hers, skilled and masterful.

At first she held herself stiffly, but, pressing her back against the door, he kissed her until her head was spinning and her knees turned to jelly.

Feeling her slender body grow limp, he swept her up into his arms and, his lips still clinging closely, carried her back to the couch. Laying her on it, he sat down by her side, effectively trapping her there while he continued to kiss her.

Even though it was evident that she no longer had the breath to scream, it was a little while before he raised his head.

When, her senses reeling and feeling as if her soul had lost its way, she opened dazed eyes, he was staring down at her, an odd expression on his face.

His voice husky, he said, 'You may look like a child, but it was a woman I held in my arms, a woman who, in spite of that air of untouched innocence, responded to my kisses…'

She wanted to deny that she had responded, but couldn't. She hadn't been able to help herself. Though she had tried hard to resist him, the moment his lips had touched hers she had been lost.

'How old are you?'

'Seventeen,' she whispered. Wishing she was older.

'And still a virgin, I think?'

Quite a few of her school friends had been only too eager to lose their virginity to any boy who showed an interest, but Gail had been brought up to have good morals, to respect herself.

Though several boys had tried their luck, put off by their immature fumbling, their wet lips and sweaty palms, she had never even been tempted. Such coolness had earned her the nickname of Miss Icicles.

But, flat on her back and at a disadvantage, stung by what

she took as scorn, she scoffed, 'In this day and age? You must be joking.'

He lifted his shoulders in a shrug. 'I suppose, despite that virginal air, I should have expected it. A potential beauty like you must have attracted any number of boys.'

'Please don't make fun of me,' she said in a stifled voice.

'I'm not making fun of you.' His voice was dark and serious. 'Unlike Rona, you're obviously a late developer. At the moment you're like a rosebud that's too tightly curled. However, in a year or so…'

He let the words tail off and, getting to his feet, took both her hands in his and pulled her into a sitting position.

Feeling bemused and elated and self-conscious all at the same time, she straightened her skirt and jacket and looked anywhere but at him.

Sitting down again, his eyes on her flushed face, he said quizzically, 'Now, you know what happens if you threaten to scream; let's have an answer to my question. What is Rona up to that she doesn't want me to know about?'

'She's spending the weekend on a yacht,' Gail said in a rush.

'Well, if she wants to join a weekend party on a yacht, why didn't she tell me?' Then, his green eyes narrowing, he demanded, 'Whose yacht?'

'Johnny Chator's,' she told him reluctantly.

He cursed. 'No wonder she didn't want me to know. Still, there's said to be safety in numbers… So long as she takes care not to be left alone with him—'

Catching sight of Gail's expressive face, he stopped short. Then, with dawning comprehension, 'Don't tell me… This is going to be a private party, a party just for two.'

When she failed to deny it, he exploded, 'Damn it, Chator's more than twice her age and he's got a reputation for having some nasty habits.'

Standing quickly, he demanded, 'What time is she planning to leave?'

'She's already gone.' Seeing that he was genuinely concerned, she added, 'But I'm sure she can take care of herself—'

His face impatient, Zane brushed her words aside. 'Though Rona *appears* to know her way around, in some respects she's never really grown up; she's still something of an innocent…'

Then, shortly, 'Judging by your expression, you don't agree.'

'No, I don't,' Gail said quietly.

'Well, no doubt we see things in a different way. Rona may seem sophisticated and worldly to you, but at heart she's still Daddy's little girl.

'That's why she was so upset when he married for a second time. She was jealous of his new wife, jealous of you, afraid she was going to lose out…'

With a groan, he sat down and ran his hands through his hair. 'I hate to think of her alone with a swine like Chator.' Then, in obvious frustration, 'She can't have realized just what she might be letting herself in for.'

Gail gritted her teeth. 'I think she does.'

Zane's head came up. 'Then why on earth did she agree to go?'

Gail bit her bottom lip. 'She's hoping to find a rich husband and—'

'She's what?' His eyes blazed with fury.

Frightened by his anger, she whispered, 'Hoping to find a rich husband.'

'And she thinks Chator might fit the bill?'

'Yes,' Gail said miserably.

Zane shook his head, incredulous. 'Doesn't she know that he sheds his wives faster than most men shed their mistresses?'

'Yes, she knows.'

'What makes you so sure?'

'She said so.'

'Tell me exactly what she said.'

Agitation bringing her to her feet, she stammered, 'I—I really don't…'

He rose and, looming over her menacingly, ordered, 'Start from the beginning and tell me what Rona said.'

Bowing to a will-power stronger than hers, Gail took a deep, uneven breath. Then, quietly and with obvious truth, she repeated as well as she could remember exactly what Rona had told her.

While she spoke, Zane stood quietly, his eyes fixed on her face, making no attempt to interrupt.

When she had finished, a white line appearing round his mouth, he said bleakly, 'And here I was thinking Rona and I had a future together, but now it's clear that all the time she was just using me while she looked for someone with more money.' He laughed bitterly.

It was obvious that he was furiously angry, but mingled with that anger was the hurt and pain of disillusionment and loss.

Gail's heart went out to him as, for perhaps the first time, she appreciated that his feelings for Rona had gone far beyond mere sexual attraction.

Grieved to have been the one to tell him, she whispered, 'I wish I hadn't said anything.'

'Well, I suppose I had to know some time what a poor sucker I've been.'

His bitterness, and the desolate look on his face, shocked her. She rose to her feet and, tears gathering in her clear dark grey eyes, she whispered, 'I'm sorry. Truly I am.'

Standing on tiptoe, she made the bravest move she'd ever had the courage to make and went to kiss him, but he moved his head slightly and her kiss brushed only the corner of his mouth.

Flustered and embarrassed, she took a hasty step back,

caught her heel in the rug and, completely off balance, would have fallen if he hadn't gathered her to him.

The close contact with his hard, muscular frame took her breath away and turned every single bone in her body to water.

With no thought of the past or the future, conscious only of the love that filled her heart and the desire to comfort him, she melted against him and lifted her face blindly to his.

When his lips touched hers, she made a sound like a sigh and opened her mouth to him.

At first his kiss was deliberately hard and punitive but, instead of scaring her, as he'd half expected, she put her arms around his neck and, melting against him, returned his kisses with a passionate warmth that sent him up in flames.

At length, lifting his head, he ordered harshly, 'You'd better go.'

When, sensing the need in him, she made no move to obey, he said, 'Look, I'm only human, so unless you're prepared to end up in my bed, you'd better do as I say.'

He started to push her away but she clung closer, whispering, 'I want to stay.'

'Don't be a little fool,' he said roughly. 'Tomorrow you'll regret it.'

'I won't. I love you,' she said quietly and pressed her slender body against his.

As though his self-control had snapped, with scant regard for her youth and inexperience, he began to strip off first her clothes and then his own.

Laying her down on the carpet, he trailed his touch along her body. She shivered in response, begging him to make love to her there and then.

For perhaps the first time in his life, his passion fuelled more by anger than desire, he took without caring overmuch what he gave back.

Even so, Gail was swept away by his kisses, the touch of his skin on hers, and he carried her on a flight to the heavens, leaving her limp and quivering in the aftermath of such ecstacy.

But, though he had given her the kind of delight she had never even imagined, she felt a keen sense of loss, of sadness. While to her their lovemaking had been exquisite, she knew that he felt no tenderness or caring towards her.

Although what had she expected? She had thrown herself at him and, driven by anger and pain that the woman he loved didn't care, he had taken what she'd so freely offered.

But on the floor, as though she was just a common little slut, as though he couldn't bear to take her to the bed that Rona would have occupied.

She was filled with shame and humiliation, a feeling of disbelief that she could have acted so out of character and, rather than have to face him, she wanted to curl up and die.

When he rose to his feet she was still lying there motionless, the curly tendrils of blonde hair spread around her, her eyes shut tightly, her long, thick lashes like dark fans on her cheeks.

In his arms she had been all woman but, with her slender body and small breasts, she looked childlike and vulnerable, and, remembering her little gasp of pain at his first strong thrust, he felt callous and cruel.

But when he would have drawn back, she had tightened her arms around his neck, whispering urgently, 'It's all right. It's all right.'

Now, however, seeing the tears that squeezed themselves beneath her closed lids and trickled down her face in tracks of shiny wetness, he knew it wasn't and cursed himself savagely.

Angry with her for misleading him, for throwing away her virginity, and furious with himself for taking it, he began to pull on his clothes.

He was buttoning his shirt when, chilled and shivering, she scrambled to her feet.

Seeing his eyes fixed on her, she crossed her thin arms over her small breasts.

He found himself absurdly touched by her attempt at modesty and that made him even angrier.

His mouth compressing, he gathered up her things and, tossing them on to the couch, said curtly, 'You'd better get dressed and get out of here.'

As, with pathetic dignity, she began to pull on her clothes and shoes, he saw that her hands were shaking and, obeying the temptation to lash out, observed caustically, 'I should thank you for trying to console me.'

Only too aware that what had started as an attempt to comfort him had gone horribly wrong, she whispered, 'I'm sorry.'

'Why be sorry?' Now he was being intentionally cruel. 'Presumably you got what you wanted. But if you're hoping to take Rona's place, you'll have to think again. Inexperienced schoolgirls just out for a thrill aren't my style.'

Flayed, mortified, she snatched up her bag and jacket and, blinded by tears, fled.

Knowing she couldn't go on to the theatre club as if nothing had happened, she began to walk aimlessly, seeing nothing and uncaring of where she went, until at long last she succeeded in getting the worst of her misery and agitation under control.

Clouds had gathered and it was starting to rain—big, heavy drops of summer rain that plopped on to the sidewalk, making dollar-sized rings in the dust and the air smell of ozone.

Finding herself outside her own apartment building, like someone on automatic pilot, she took out her card-key and let herself in.

She was crossing the lobby when the sight of three men approaching stopped her dead in her tracks.

An angry-looking Zane was in the middle, flanked by Patrick and a burly policeman.

'Miss Abbey,' the security guard exclaimed, 'you're just the person we want. This man says his name is Zane Lorenson and he's a friend of your sister's; he was seen loitering outside your apartment…'

So he'd come to check that she'd spoken the truth, that Rona really had gone.

'When I asked him how he got into the building, he said your sister had given him a key, but he was unable to produce it, and there was no one home to verify his statement—'

Appearing to be holding on to his patience only with an effort, Zane broke in, 'I've already explained that I'd just mislaid it and that the regular security staff know me well.'

As though he hadn't spoken, Patrick went on, 'He then admitted that he'd walked in with one of the tenants. He said he was visiting you, but I knew you'd gone out, so—'

'For heaven's sake—' Zane appealed directly to Gail '—tell him you know me.'

Sounding surprised, the security guard asked, 'Can you vouch for him, Miss Abbey?'

Still raw and bleeding from the way Zane had humiliated her, the way he'd said, 'Inexperienced schoolgirls just out for a thrill aren't my style', and at that moment hating him for it and wanting to hit back, she shook her head and said jerkily, 'I'm afraid I can't.'

She saw the icy anger in his green eyes before she turned and hurried away.

By the time she reached her apartment, already bitterly regretting what she'd done, she was shaking so much that she could hardly open the door.

Feeling sick and hollow inside, she went straight to her room but, too agitated to sit down, she began to pace restlessly, going over and over the little scene in her mind.

Recalling that look of cold fury in Zane's eyes, she shivered.

He wasn't the sort of man who would take kindly to being made a fool of and sooner or later she would have to face him and answer to him for what she'd done…

The sound of the outer door opening and closing penetrated her thoughts and brought her heart into her mouth. Had she closed it properly in her agitated state?

But when she plucked up enough courage to go and look, it was her mother.

'You're back early…' They spoke in unison.

Catching sight of the bruises on her mother's face, Gail asked urgently, 'What have you done? How did you come to hurt yourself?'

The clear grey eyes that were so like her daughter's filled with tears. 'Earlier tonight Martin came round to the Shelter and caused a terrible scene. He was drunk and when I wouldn't leave with him he went mad.'

Elizabeth put a hand to her bruised face. 'It took three of the helpers to throw him out. Father Delaney brought me home.'

The tears spilt over and ran down her cheeks. 'I've had more than enough. I've decided to leave him. We'll go back to England.'

'But how will we manage?'

'Harriet knows there've been problems with the marriage, and the last time she wrote she said that if ever we wanted to go home we could stay with her for as long as we needed…'

Though Gail hadn't seen her aunt for several years she had always been extremely fond of her and the thought of the warm welcome they were sure to receive cheered her up considerably.

'…And I can get a job of some kind.'

'I'll get one too.'

Elizabeth shook her head. 'You've only got another year at school, and I want you to go on to college and finish your education.'

'Oh, but—'

'We'll manage somehow.'

'Are you sure you're doing the right thing?'

'Absolutely sure.' Then, a shade anxiously, 'You don't want to stay in the States, do you?'

'No. I love New York, but I've never really been happy living with Martin and Rona.'

'No, God forgive me, I know you haven't. The marriage was a sad mistake that we've both paid dearly for.

'I should never have married him, but I was lonely, I missed your dad, and Martin was a good-looking man who could be very kind and charming when he wanted to be. By the time I realized just what he was like, it was too late.'

'How soon do you want to leave?'

Dashing away the tears, Elizabeth said, 'As soon as possible. To save any further trouble, perhaps we could pack now and start for the airport before he gets home.'

As far as Gail was concerned, to be able to go at once and leave all the trauma behind was the answer to a prayer. 'Yes, let's,' she agreed eagerly.

A little over an hour later, they were in a taxi heading for Queens and JFK airport…

Just then Zane's voice broke into her thoughts and made her jump. She was forced to put the past behind her and remember why she was here. 'Sorry, I was miles away.'

'Reminiscing?' He had an unnerving knack of appearing to read her mind.

'No,' she denied quickly.

'Contemplating the future?'

She shook her head. 'I was just thinking about travelling in general.'

He sat back and observed the tension on her face. 'Earlier this morning you mentioned that you'd been to Europe?'

'I'm afraid they were only package holidays,' she explained depreciatingly.

'To one of the Costas?'

She shook her head. 'France and Switzerland a couple of times, and once to Austria.'

'Alone?'

'With a friend.' She sipped her drink, avoiding eye contact with him.

'Male or female?'

He watched her generous mouth tighten, before she asked shortly, 'Does the sex make any difference?'

His lips twitched, as if he was trying not to smile, before he answered, 'It might well to the people involved.'

'I mean, I don't see why you're asking. Why it makes any difference to you.'

'It gives me an insight into your character…'

Watching her like a hawk, he added, 'You see, I like to *know* my PA inside out. What kind of woman she is, how she handles her life, her attitude to the opposite sex, what makes her tick…'

CHAPTER FIVE

FEELING rather like some specimen on the end of a cruel pin, Gail repressed a shudder.

'So was it male or female?'

Rattled by his arrogance, she demanded, 'How can you be certain I'll speak the truth?'

'Because you have a very expressive face and I can tell when you're lying.

'Which was it?'

'Male,' she told him boldly.

He smiled wolfishly. 'I'm not sure I believe you.'

'As I consider that my private life is my own business, I don't—' She broke off, her grey eyes sparkling with anger.

'Go on,' he urged, 'say it.'

'I don't much care whether you believe me or not.'

'That's my girl!' he applauded. 'I do like a touch of spirit in a woman.'

Then with no change of tone, 'Do you speak any other language?'

A little surprised by what seemed an abrupt change of subject, she replied, 'During my last year at school I learnt French and a little German.'

'You don't speak Italian?'

She shook her head.

'Have you been to Italy before?'

Puzzled by the way he'd phrased the question, she said, 'No, I've never been to Italy. I've always wanted to go, but Jo preferred somewhere that would hopefully be a little cooler.'

'It can get very hot there in summer,' he agreed.

'I understand it can get quite hot in Manhattan,' she said carefully.

'Hot and airless at times,' he admitted. 'Though it's one of my favourite places.'

Wondering how long it would take a small plane to cross the Atlantic, how long they would have to be cooped up together like this, she asked, 'What time will we get to New York?'

He raised a dark brow. 'What makes you think we're going to New York?'

Nonplussed, she stammered, 'Well, I—I understood your offices were there.'

'So they are. However, that doesn't happen to be where we're going.'

With a stirring of unease, she asked, 'Then where are we going?'

'Italy. Tuscany, to be precise.'

'Tuscany?' she echoed, the feeling of unease increasing tenfold.

Apparently noting that unease, he queried, 'Does where we're going make any difference?'

She bit her lip. 'It just seems a strange location for a business trip.'

'Ah, but this isn't an ordinary business trip—'

Thoroughly alarmed now, she demanded, 'If it isn't a business trip, why do you need a PA?'

'I said an *ordinary* business trip. For a while now there's been some unfinished business I've been wanting to deal with. The kind of business that makes your presence essential.'

There was an strange note in his voice, a nuance, the faintest undercurrent of…what?

Menace?

Shivering, she told herself not to be a fool. She was letting her imagination run away with her again.

'I thought it might be a good idea to get to know one another before we start work in earnest, so I decided to combine business with pleasure, and Tuscany is the ideal place to do that.'

'Oh…' she said hollowly.

'I know you share my liking for Abruzzi's landscapes but, other than that, do you know much about the region?'

Making an effort to keep her voice steady, she answered, 'Not a great deal, I'm afraid, and hardly anything about the countryside. Though, from the paintings and photographs I've seen, it appears to be really beautiful.'

He laughed. 'Yes, it is. It's varied and colourful, with vineyards and olive groves and field upon field of golden sunflowers.

'Of course the towns and cities are picturesque and historical, well worth visiting. Florence, Pisa, Lucca, Siena…' Gail was entranced by his words, wanting to know more about all the amazing places he'd been.

'It's around Siena that you'll see the distinctive orangey-red earth that's the origin of the painting pigment burnt sienna, which was used a great deal by the Renaissance painters.

'But away from the big towns and cities it's quiet and peaceful, with villas and farmhouses dotted about, little hamlets and medieval walled towns perched on the hilltops…'

Warmed by his genuine enthusiasm, which somehow made him seem more human, she relaxed a little. 'I hope I'll get a chance to see it.'

'Oh, you will,' he assured her.

'Where exactly are we heading for?'

She was expecting him to say Florence or one of the other major cities, when, his clear dark green eyes fixed on her face, he queried, 'Have you ever heard of Montecino?'

She shook her head.

'It's one of the small medieval hilltop towns I just mentioned…'

Hoping against hope that she had misunderstood, she said, 'You don't mean that's where we'll be staying?'

'Not in the town itself. I have a villa about two miles away as the crow flies. It's a bit off the beaten track, but the scenery is magnificent.'

Her heart sank like a stone.

Had they been staying at a hotel in Florence with plenty of other people around, it would have been bad enough. But there was no way she could cope alone with him in some remote villa.

As she struggled to hide her alarm, Zane added cheerfully, 'Don't worry, it's not completely isolated. The nearest hamlet is only about three quarters of a mile away in the valley.

'Villa Severo stands on a hilltop, with wonderful views over the countryside. The original building—part castle, part house—dates from the mid-seventeenth century and was virtually in ruins when I bought it.

'But it's now been completely rebuilt with all mod cons, including a swimming pool. I think you'll like it,' he added, a note of quiet pride in his voice.

It might have wonderful views, Gail thought bleakly, but if she had had the faintest idea where he was intending to bring her, she would never have come in a million years. How could she spend time so isolated and in such close proximity to Zane Lorenson?

This whole thing had gone disastrously wrong, and when

they reached the airport she would use her credit card and get
the first flight back home.

She was about to tell him so when caution made her bite her
tongue. It wasn't that she was chicken, she assured herself. But
now, while they were still cooped up together, wasn't the time
to tell him she was opting out, especially as he'd made it quite
clear that he wanted her with him.

Though *why* he needed a PA when presumably in such an
out of the way place he would be doing his business by
computer, she couldn't begin to imagine.

Made uncomfortable by the possibilities that thought engen-
dered, she pushed it resolutely away and tried to concentrate
on how best to explain her change of heart.

After a while she sighed, knowing that however she explained it he wasn't likely to take kindly to the idea. But once
she had her luggage and her passport back, if the worst came
to the worst she could simply refuse point-blank to go any
further.

There was a tap and the steward came in to announce,
'Captain Giardino asked me to say that, unless you want to take
the controls yourself, he'll be coming in to land in about ten
minutes.'

So Zane was a pilot too, Gail thought. Well, she might have
expected it. He was the kind of man who could do anything he
set his mind to.

'Thanks, Jarvis. Please tell the Captain to go right ahead.'

When the steward had gone, as casually as possible, Gail
asked, 'Are we landing at Florence or Pisa?'

'Neither…'

So presumably they were landing at Bologna.

She was waiting for Zane to confirm that, when he went on
calmly, 'We'll be putting down at Voste, a small, privately
owned airfield…'

A small private airfield rather than the big airport she had anticipated...

Feeling like some fugitive who, dreaming of escape, had just seen the bars of the cage close round her, she stared at him in complete consternation.

'There's no need to look quite so fraught. It has a more than adequate runway, a well-trained staff and a first class safety record.'

Thankful that he had put her agitation down to being scared of flying, she made a determined effort to pull herself together.

As it seemed she had no alternative but to see this thing through, she must endeavour to keep her cool and make the best of it.

Taking a deep breath, she asked, 'Why did you choose to land there?'

'When I fly to Tuscany we always land at Voste. It's very convenient, just a few miles north of the villa, and Lorenzo da Voste and his wife, Lucia, happen to be very good friends of mine.

'I would have liked you to have met him and his family— he has three young children—but unfortunately they're in Capri at the moment...'

Apparently intent on taking Gail's mind off the landing, Zane talked easily until they had touched down and taxied to a halt in front of a series of hangars and prefabricated buildings.

Several uniformed staff appeared and, while a set of steps was wheeled into place, the steward opened the door of the plane.

Zane pulled on his jacket and picked up his briefcase. 'If you'll excuse me for a moment, I've got a spot of official business to attend to.' Striding down the steps, he disappeared into what looked like an office.

He was back quite quickly, but by that time Gail had collected her belongings and the luggage had been unloaded and transferred to a white open-topped car standing close by.

The late afternoon sky was a cloudless Mediterranean blue, the sun beat down and the oven heat of the tarmac burnt through the thin soles of her court shoes as she was escorted down the steps and to the waiting car.

When she had been settled in the front passenger seat, Zane put her jacket and his briefcase into the back and moved away to have a word with a group of men.

It immediately became clear that he spoke fluent Italian. But then he would, she thought a shade bitterly, while not knowing the language was bound to put her at a disadvantage.

Seeing Captain Giardino join Zane and the little group, she wondered if he would be coming with them and staying at the villa.

She fervently hoped so. It would be a comfort to have another person there, especially someone who could speak English. And where else would he stay?

The airfield was situated on a flat, fertile plain with green, rolling hills on either side. Beyond the white control tower she could see the silvery-green shimmer of an olive grove and away in the distance were stands of what looked like chestnut trees.

To the right, about halfway up the hill, was a large terraced villa with colour-washed walls. It was the only house in sight.

Everywhere was peaceful. Sunshine fell golden as honey on her bare arms and the chirping of cicadas filled the drowsy air. Her worries momentarily fading, Gail lifted her face to the sun and closed her eyes.

The previous night's lack of sleep starting to catch up with her, she was just drifting off when she heard Zane's voice close by.

Her eyes flew open.

He was approaching the car and talking into a mobile phone.

'*Sono qui in vacanza… Si… Quando?… Si, si, bene… Ciao, Paolo.*'

She was wondering if Paolo was a business acquaintance when, dropping the mobile into his jacket pocket, he said regretfully, 'I'm sorry if I disturbed you. That's the first time today I've seen you looking anything like relaxed.'

'I was just enjoying the sunshine.'

'I think I'll join you.' He took off his jacket and tossed it on to the back seat of the car before removing his tie and dropping it into one of the car's glove pockets.

When he'd unfastened the top few buttons of his shirt and rolled up his sleeves to expose muscular arms, he said with satisfaction, 'Now I *feel* as if I'm on holiday…

'How does your first glimpse of Tuscany strike you?'

'It must be a lovely place to live,' she said, and meant it.

'Lucia and Lorenzo think so; that's why they much prefer to stay here—' he indicated the colour-washed villa '—even though they have big houses in Florence and Rome.

'While Lorenzo is a direct descendent of one of the Grand Dukes of Tuscany, and extremely wealthy, he's very down-to-earth and he and Lucia much prefer to live simply.

'Although they've a house full of servants, Lucia always does her own cooking. Her La Ribollita, one of the most famous of Tuscan soups, is the best I've ever tasted…'

When he slid behind the wheel and started the ignition with a soft roar, Gail glanced around. She could see the airfield staff going about their business, but there was no sign of the pilot.

'Where's Captain Giardino?' she asked quickly.

Zane lifted a dark brow. 'Why do you ask?'

'Well, I… I just wondered where he was staying.'

'He's staying at the villa, as usual.'

Her heart lifted.

As Zane put the car into gear and they moved off, she asked, 'Aren't you going to wait for him?'

She saw the corner of his mouth twitch before, indicating the house on the hillside, he told her, 'I meant *that* villa. Carlo, who is distantly related to Lucia, always stays there whether the family are home or not.'

'Oh…'

Zane gave her a glinting sidelong glance. 'You sound disappointed.'

'Not at all,' she said stiffly.

With smooth mockery, he went on, 'And, before you ask about Jarvis, he's going back to Montecino with one of the mechanics. I hope it won't shock you, but he has a lady friend there.'

Her mouth tight, Gail said nothing.

At the entrance to the airfield the security staff gave Zane a friendly wave, which he returned, and the tall gates in the chain-link fence were swung open for them.

Leaving the airfield, they followed a narrow, winding road along the valley floor. Everywhere was quiet and peaceful. Once they had picked up speed, the balmy breeze of their passing stroked her cheeks like soft fingers and ruffled her hair. Glancing sideways at him, she saw that the tough, hard-headed businessman had gone. With his shirt open at the neck and the breeze flicking a lock of dark hair over his forehead, he looked relaxed and carefree, almost boyish, not the ruthless tycoon she knew him to be.

Seeing him like that made her heart feel as if it were being squeezed in a giant fist, and she sighed for what might have been.

A mile or so along the valley, they passed a small picturesque village before they began to climb the wooded hillside. The scenery was lovely but, apprehensive about what lay ahead, she was unable to relax and enjoy it.

Showing he never missed a thing, Zane asked, 'What's wrong?'

She shook her head. 'Nothing.'

'Don't lie to me,' he said crisply. 'You've been uptight from the word go.'

When she remained silent, he gave her a quick, searching glance and asked, 'Why did you want to work for me?'

The unexpected question jolted her and she stammered, 'I—I needed a job.'

'I'm rather surprised The Manton Group didn't offer you one.'

'There wasn't an opening for a PA.'

'How did you come to hear that *I* needed one?'

After a moment's frantic thought, she said, 'I found out from the agency.'

'And you saw Mrs Rogers.'

It was a statement, not a question, but she answered, 'Yes.'

'When I spoke to Mrs Rogers myself, she told me you were very keen to have the job.'

'Yes, I—I was.'

When she said nothing further, he pursued, 'So you were pleased when you got it?'

'Well…yes.'

'In that case, why have you been like a cat on a hot tin roof ever since?'

Her common sense telling her that it was no use trying to deny it, she said, 'I couldn't help but wonder if I'd made a mistake. If I should have accepted your offer.'

'Why? Because the interview wasn't the standard, polite kind you were expecting?'

'It was partly that… But then everything happened so quickly, and I must admit that having to come away so suddenly, before I'd had time to settle in, threw me somewhat.'

'Well, the die's cast and it's too late for regrets, so I suggest you try and relax a little.'

He was right about the die being cast.

That being the case, the last thing she wanted to do was make him suspicious, so somehow she must try to do as he said and play the part of a normal PA.

In a little while they reached a pair of handsome wrought iron gates set in an old wall. They were standing invitingly open.

The serpentine drive ran between terraced gardens that, with varied trees and shrubs and masses of flowering creepers tumbling over the retaining walls, were a riot of colour.

They had rounded the last bend before the house itself came into view. As Zane stopped the car in a cobbled courtyard, she caught her breath.

It was starkly beautiful, more so than she could ever have imagined. No wonder he was proud of it.

Perhaps because it had been recently rebuilt, and he had referred to it as a villa, she had expected something colour-washed and stuccoed that appeared relatively modern, but this place had an almost medieval air about it.

With a huge arched doorway and arched windows set in high walls built of pale random stone, the place looked more like a small castle than a house.

It appeared to be built on several different levels and boasted a jumble of pantiled roofs at various angles, some with chimneys. At one end, incorporated in the building, was a big round tower with a squat, candle-snuffer roof.

'Like it?' he asked.

'It's absolutely wonderful,' she said sincerely. 'You must have had a brilliant architect to design something like this.'

He shook his head. 'It wasn't designed by my architect. I already knew exactly what I wanted, as I'd been lucky enough to come across a series of old paintings that showed what the original building had looked like before it started to fall into disrepair.

'Where my architect proved his worth was in making detailed plans from the rough sketches I'd had done.'

He restarted the car and turned right through an archway into another courtyard at the rear, where a heavy studded door was standing open.

There were tubs of scarlet and white geraniums and, incongruously, a battered motor scooter with a pillion seat propped against one of the walls.

Zane brought the car to a halt and, as he helped Gail out, a woman appeared in the doorway.

'This is Maria Colasanti,' he told her, 'my caretaker-cum-housekeeper and the lady who manages to organize everything.'

Dark-haired and buxom, dressed in serviceable country clothes, Maria looked more like a farmer's wife than a housekeeper.

As though to confirm that thought, he added, 'Her husband, who worked on a nearby farm, died just as this place was being finished, so she was pleased to take the job. She's turned out to be a treasure.'

'*Buonasera,* Signor Lorenson,' the woman exclaimed, showing strong white teeth as she smiled broadly.

'*Buonasera,* Maria,' he greeted her. '*Comesta?*'

'*Va bene,* Signor Lorenson…'

As Zane introduced the two women, who nodded and smiled at each other, a sturdily built youth appeared and, giving the newcomers a shy smile, began to take the luggage from the car.

The likeness between the young man and the older woman was so marked that Gail presumed they must be closely related.

As though echoing her thoughts once again, Zane said, 'This

is Angelo, Maria's eldest son. Apart from providing necessary transport, he's a big help around the place.'

Retrieving their belongings from the back seat, Zane handed Gail her jacket. His own jacket over his arm and his briefcase in his hand, he left the car where it was and led the way inside, chatting to the housekeeper as they went.

The large hall was light and airy and open-plan, with rustic archways, long windows and an elegant chestnut wood stair-case running up the middle.

Turning to Gail, he explained, 'You'll find the three princi-pal rooms are situated in the tower. The library-cum-study is on the ground floor—' he indicated a door to the left of the stairs '—the living room is on the floor above and the master bedroom is on the floor above that.'

Casually, he added, 'Your bedroom is next door to mine. If you follow Maria, she'll show you the way.'

As the housekeeper smiled and nodded, he added, 'When you've had time to unpack and freshen up, make your way down the spiral stairs to the living room and we'll have a drink on the terrace.'

A moment later he disappeared into his study.

Glancing around her curiously, and in spite of everything liking what she saw, Gail accompanied the housekeeper up the staircase, Angelo following behind with her luggage.

At the top of the stairs, the landing was lit by a row of handsome oriel windows which, despite the new woodwork, gave it a much older feel.

They climbed the next flight and, having crossed an identi-cal landing, turned down a wide passageway where Maria showed her into a large room adjacent to the tower.

The windows, curtained in off-white muslin, were open wide, letting in warm air that carried the combined scent of rosemary and lavender.

Glancing out, Gail saw there were magnificent views across the valley, while through the trees she could make out glimpses of the road they had come up by, winding down the hillside.

When Angelo had placed her case carefully on a low chest, Gail said, '*Grazie,*' one of the few words of Italian she knew, and smiled at mother and son.

They returned the smile and departed.

The room, with its *en suite* bathroom, was light and pleasant, with modern furniture and a comfortable-looking double bed. Though Zane had assured her that the villa had 'all mod cons' there was no phone.

Her heart sank.

But surely there would be phones downstairs. If she was careful to chose her moment, she might be able to make a quick call to Paul to let him know where she was and what was happening.

She opened her case and set aside fresh underwear, a silk shift, a pair of strappy sandals and her night things and toiletries, before transferring the rest of her belongings to the chest of drawers and the big walk-in wardrobe.

Then, stripping off her clothes, she placed the chain that held Paul's ring on the dressing table and went into the luxurious bathroom.

A towelling bathrobe had been laid out ready, along with piles of soft towels and a wide array of expensive toiletries. But, after glancing through them, she decided that she preferred her own modest apple blossom, which she had liked and used for years.

Though the shower was refreshing, even enjoyable, the thought of the several hours that she would have to spend alone with Zane before she could go to bed filled her with dismay. But the evening had to be faced and, hopefully, she could plead tiredness and escape early.

She was emerging from the bathroom when a sound like an angry hornet drew her over to the window and she was just in time to catch sight of a motor scooter on the road down to the valley.

It seemed that Angelo was going out for the evening.

But that still left Maria, and though she couldn't communicate with the housekeeper verbally, it was nice to know there was someone else in the house.

When she was dressed, she put on the merest touch of make-up to boost her morale and brushed out her dark, silky hair before taking it up again into a businesslike coil.

Then, after a moment's hesitation, feeling in need of the reassurance it offered, she dropped the thin gold chain over her head and tucked Paul's ring down the front of her bra.

A quick glance in the cheval mirror convinced her that she looked cool and composed and, determined to stay that way, she set off to face the evening.

A door in the tower gave access to the spiral stairs that Zane had mentioned. Beautifully designed, they were made of the same lovely chestnut wood as the main staircase and had an ornate metal hand rail.

The high heels of her sandals clicking lightly on the steps, she made her way down to an attractive and spacious living room with a huge arched fireplace built of pale random stone and filled with flowers.

Cushioned chairs and couches covered in linen that shaded from oatmeal through to mushroom were grouped in front of the hearth, while the walls were painted a rich, glowing burnt ochre.

Apprised of her coming, Zane was waiting at the bottom of the stairs, his dark, well-shaped head tilted back a little to watch her descent.

He had changed into casual stone-coloured trousers and an

olive-green silk shirt open at the throat. Freshly shaven, his hair still damp from the shower, he looked so devastatingly attractive that her heart began to beat faster.

As she reached the bottom he gave her a little smile and silently held out his hand.

Like someone caught in a dream, someone who had no choice but to play the part allotted to her, she put hers into it.

She instantly regretted it.

A kind of electric shock made her whole body tingle and she snatched her hand away as if it had been burnt.

She regretted that too. The involuntary reaction had been much too revealing.

She heard his soft, amused chuckle as he put a hand at her waist and, walking slightly behind her, began to steer her towards a pair of open French windows.

As they reached them, his hands closed lightly around her upper arms, stopping her dead in her tracks. She felt the warmth of his breath on the side of her neck as, bending forward, his lips almost brushing her ear, he murmured, 'You smell as fresh and delightful as a spring morning. When we met it was one of the first things I noticed about you.

'Once upon a time,' he added softly, 'I knew a girl who wore that same perfume.'

His words made her blood turn to ice in her veins and, standing frozen with horror, she wondered frantically if he knew who she was and, intent on punishing her, had been playing with her like a cat played with a mouse.

Or was she letting her own guilt and awareness undermine her?

Somehow she found her voice and said jerkily, 'That's not surprising. It's very common.'

Without further comment, he released her and together they stepped out on to a semicircular stone terrace with panoramic views across the peaceful countryside that were even more spectacular than the ones from her bedroom window.

The impression that the terrace—with its wrought iron balustrade—was suspended in space was almost overpowering until she saw that it was supported by pillars and that wrought iron steps led down to the courtyard beneath.

On a low table was a tray of drinks and a pair of cushioned loungers issued a mute invitation.

When she was settled in one of them, Zane asked, 'So what's it going to be?'

Her coolness and composure gone, and feeling in need of a bit of Dutch courage, she threw caution to the winds. 'I'd rather like a gin and tonic, please.'

'Ice and lemon?'

She nodded. 'Please.'

As he mixed the drinks, in an effort to steady herself, she looked around her.

Away to the west, the sun was just slipping below the horizon and the *contre-jour* lighting and the long purple shadows made the scenery even more dramatic.

One or two wispy ribbons of cloud had appeared in a sky of aquamarine flecked with palest pink and a balmy evening breeze had sprung up, caressing her forehead and playing with a fine strand of her hair that had escaped.

Had the circumstances been other than they were, she would have looked forward greatly to staying in this lovely isolated spot.

But, as it was, she would have happily swapped all the peace and serenity for the noise and dust and bustling crowds of one of the big towns or cities.

Though surely she would be better able to face the thought of being at the Villa Severo, virtually alone with Zane, when she had managed to talk to Paul and, hopefully, caught up on last night's lost sleep.

CHAPTER SIX

'HERE we are—one gin and tonic.'

Zane's voice broke into her thoughts and she turned to find he was by her side, holding out a glass.

Taking it, she said composedly, 'Thank you.'

'Try it and see if it's to your taste.'

As he spoke, as if determined to destroy any attempt at composure, he brushed the tendril of hair away from her cheek and tucked it behind her ear.

His action turned the intended sip into a gulp and she was forced to cough.

'Not too strong, I trust?' Though his expression was bland, innocent, she thought she could detect an air of satisfaction, almost triumph.

'No... No, it's fine, thank you.'

Telling herself vexedly that she would have to exercise a great deal more self-control, she took refuge once again in staring out over the countryside while she sipped more carefully.

Zane sat down next to her.

Much too close for comfort.

Stretching his long legs indolently, his eyes fixed on the rolling hills, he began to drink his own whisky soda.

Almost as soon as the sun had vanished from view, the sky started to lose its brightness and a purple velvet dusk began to creep stealthily out of hiding.

The cypresses stood out, tall and dark and straight, against the deep blue sky, a myriad stars began to appear and gauzy-winged bats flitted around in the silky air.

'Night falls quickly here,' Zane remarked. Giving her a little intimate smile, he added with evident satisfaction, 'It's taken some planning, but I've been looking forward to this.'

'To what?' she asked sharply. Too sharply.

'To being on holiday.'

Of course. What else could he have meant?

Trying to sound more relaxed, she observed, 'Though it's nearly dark, it's still beautifully warm.'

'Yes, though at Severo, I'm pleased to say, we don't have the kind of intense heat and humidity that Florence can have, the kind that keeps you awake at night unless you have air-conditioning.'

Softly, he added, 'Here you can make love, then lie naked and comfortable in each other's arms…'

Her throat going dry at the intimate picture his words painted, she said the first thing that came into her head. 'I haven't seen the swimming pool you mentioned earlier…'

'It's a couple of levels below us and to the left. You can't see it from here because of the overhang. There's an open-air Jacuzzi too. Ever been in one?'

'No.'

After a drifting silence, he went on, 'It's really something to sit in a Jacuzzi under the stars when the fireflies are out and the moonlit air's still warm and scented with myrtle.'

She saw the gleam of his eyes in the deepening dusk as he added, 'If you've no inhibitions about taking off your clothes, we could try it later…'

Not on your life! she thought.

She had believed Paul when he'd assured her that Zane Lorenson never mixed business with pleasure.

But out here on the dusky terrace, the setting was far too romantic, and feeling the sexual tension that seemed to stretch between them like barbed wire—a tension she had been aware of all along but had refused to acknowledge—she wondered anxiously if Paul could have been wrong.

Though if Zane could have his pick of women, and she was sure he could, why should he have designs on her? Except that, apart from Maria, she was the only woman here, and therefore available.

Though surely if he had wanted a bedmate he could have brought one…?

'Unless, as it's been a somewhat tiring day, you'd prefer to have an early night?' Zane suggested.

Even as she answered hastily, 'Yes, actually I would,' she realized that his voice had sounded light, matter-of-fact, without the slightest hint of any undue intimacy.

But perhaps *she* was the only one to experience that strong sexual awareness? Maybe all the feeling was on her side and sprang from her memories of what had happened that evening so long ago?

All she knew for certain was that it was a great deal more powerful than anything she had yet experienced with the man she loved, and whose wife she was going to be.

But that didn't matter, she told herself firmly. It was just a basic sexual attraction, an animal instinct that had nothing to do with love, nothing to do with the kind of caring relationship that she and Paul shared.

The realization that she had hardly thought about Paul since that morning, when he'd probably spent all day worrying about her, made her feel guilty.

Though *would* he have been worried about her?

Of course he would, she assured herself quickly. He loved her and was going to marry her. He'd bought her a ring.

But if he *really* loved her, would he have pressured her into doing something he knew perfectly well she didn't want to do?

Even this morning, when he must have seen how very unhappy she was, his main concern had been that she should get the job so he could put his plan of revenge into action, rather than for her.

No, she mustn't start accusing Paul of not caring just because she was finding it so difficult to cope. All he knew about her past encounter with Zane was what she had chosen to tell him, so he couldn't be blamed for not realizing just how traumatic this would be for her.

Poor Paul. Feeling ashamed of her disloyal thoughts, she decided that at bedtime, as soon as everywhere was quiet, she would creep downstairs again and call him.

She never normally rang his home phone number. Early in their relationship he'd asked her not to, saying that if by any chance she couldn't get him on his mobile then he didn't want to be disturbed.

But this time, if he didn't answer his mobile, she would. No doubt he'd be eager to know what had happened to her, and just hearing his voice would make her feel more cheerful, more secure...

'Penny for them,' Zane said.

'Sorry?'

'I was offering you a penny for your thoughts.'

'They're worth much more than that.'

'I can well believe it. You were miles away. Would you like another drink?'

'No, I wouldn't, thank you,' she said rather primly.

'So how much for your thoughts?'

'They're not for sale.'

He raised a brow nonchalantly. 'It doesn't really matter. I'm pretty sure I can guess what they were.'

The possibility brought her heart into her mouth.

He smiled as if he knew. Then, taking her empty glass, he set it down and asked, 'Ready to eat?'

She rose with alacrity. The moment dinner was over she would plead tiredness and escape to bed.

They had just reached the French windows when, although there was no sign of the housekeeper, lights flashed on in both the house and on the terrace.

'A time switch,' Zane explained, catching sight of Gail's puzzled expression.

They crossed the living room and went through an archway to a spacious oak-beamed dining room with polished floor-boards and a stone fireplace.

Glancing around anxiously, she could find no sign of a phone, nor had she been able to locate one in the living room.

When she was seated at an elegant refectory table which was set for two, Zane took a seat opposite her and reached to pour the wine.

Waiting on a central hotplate was a selection of covered dishes and a pot of coffee.

It seemed they were to serve themselves.

Unsure of her role, what Zane would expect of his PA, she hesitated, then, indicating the dishes, began, 'Would you like me to…?'

He shook his head. 'As far as I'm concerned, you're a guest. At least until we get…shall I say…better acquainted.'

Unsure how to interpret that, but somewhat reassured by his manner, she allowed herself to be helped to a tasty-looking dish that he told her was Tuscan chicken with polenta.

While they ate, he talked about Tuscany and its culture

before asking lightly, 'If we do a spot of sightseeing tomorrow, which of the towns would you like to see first?'

Breathing a sigh of relief that they were to get out and about, she said, 'I don't really mind. I've always wanted to see Florence and Pisa and, of course, Siena, which I know hardly anything about.'

He smiled at her eagerness. 'It's rated as Italy's most perfect medieval city. And the shell-shaped Campo—where the horse race takes place—is acknowledged to be one of the most beautiful squares in the world.'

'Oh, yes, I've heard of the horse race.'

'It's called the Palio, and each of the city's three districts compete...'

Rather to Gail's surprise, she found that, despite all the stress, her usual healthy appetite was back and, put more or less at ease by the normality of the conversation, she was able to enjoy her meal.

The first course was followed by freshly stewed figs served in a rich golden syrup that tasted of herbs and vanilla and was topped with ricotta.

'That was delicious,' she said as she finished the last spoonful. 'I particularly enjoyed the syrup.'

He leant forward, wiping a drizzle of syrup from her lip. When she blushed and looked away he laughed. 'It's made from Strega, a popular Italian liqueur. Both the main course and the dessert are simple to make but, like a lot of countrywomen, Maria sticks with plain, wholesome food and is an excellent cook.'

As he cleared the dishes and poured coffee for them both, he went on, 'After being used to a farmhouse range, she found the kitchen here a little daunting but she's gradually getting used to it.

'Though when I come to the villa, after the first evening I usually cook for myself.'

Surprised, Gail asked, 'Do you enjoy cooking?'

'After weeks of nothing but business, I find it very relaxing.'

Curiously, she asked, 'Are you any good at it?'

His devilish smile made her heart race. 'I've been told so. But if you'd like to judge for yourself, I'll be happy to give you a demonstration.'

Rather belatedly becoming aware of the ambiguity of the question, she started to blush furiously.

He leaned forward and touched a finger to her hot cheek, making her jump and jerk her head back. 'In order to save your maidenly blushes,' he said mockingly, 'perhaps you should have phrased that query more carefully.'

Once again she could feel the sexual tension tightening, but this time a lick of flame in those heavy-lidded green eyes left her in no doubt whatsoever that the feeling was mutual.

Desperate to find something innocuous to talk about until she could escape to bed, she harked back. 'How long has the villa been here?'

'It was finished about eighteen months ago.'

'When you first decided to build here, did you have any trouble getting water or electricity laid on?'

Though a little smile tugged at his lips, he went along with it. 'No. If I hadn't wanted a pool, at a pinch we could have managed with our own generator and water pumped from the underground spring that rises part way down the hill.

'But luckily both services already passed quite close, so that was no problem and we were able to turn the spring into a cascade.'

Then, with that unnerving ability he seemed to have to know what was in her mind, he went on evenly, 'The one thing we've had any real delay on and the one thing we're still waiting for is to have a landline phone installed.'

Through stiff lips, she queried, 'Then you don't have any phones in the house?'

'No.' He reached to refill both their coffee cups, before adding, 'But these days, with the easy availability of mobiles, a landline is no longer quite so essential.'

'What about the Internet?'

He shrugged. 'As this is primarily a holiday place, I'm quite happy to leave the outside world behind whenever possible. My mobile is all I really need.'

Without meaning to and sounding accusing, she burst out, 'My mobile's disappeared.'

'Really?' He clicked his tongue. 'How annoying for you. But if there are any calls you want to make, you can always use mine.'

While he stood by and listened, no doubt, she thought bitterly.

As though she'd spoken the words aloud, he said quizzically, 'I presume you have nothing to hide?'

Rattled afresh, she decided it would be safer to ignore the question.

After struggling for some degree of equilibrium and finally finding it, she went on, 'You said you knew how you wanted the outside of the villa to look—did you design the inside too? Or was that left in the hands of your architect?'

With a glance that seemed to acknowledge her resilience, he said, 'My architect and I worked as a team. I told him what I wanted, and he told me how I could fit it in.'

She looked around at the spacious surroundings. 'Does that include rooms for the staff?'

He shook his head. 'When I made enquiries and found I could get all the help I needed locally—a housekeeper, an odd-job man, cleaners, gardeners and a couple of men to take care of the pool—I didn't plan for any permanent live-in staff.'

He stretched his legs out in front of him, perfectly at ease. 'You see, when I'm taking a break I don't like to feel constrained. The presence of staff—no matter how discreet—is something I can well do without. I much prefer to have the house to myself.

'If I want to sunbathe on the terrace or walk about without any clothes on, I like freedom to do it. I don't want to have to take into account the feelings of a housekeeper or a maid…'

Going hot all over, her throat dry, Gail asked, 'So Maria and her son don't actually live at the villa?'

'No. Maria has a house in the village where she lives with Angelo and her three younger boys.

'As I said earlier, she's turned out to be a treasure. She organizes the cleaners, the gardeners and the men who take care of the pool and, when I'm not here, she comes up a couple of times a week to air the place and keep an eye on things.'

'But she stays when you *are* here?'

He shook his head. 'No. Angelo brings her up each day on the back of his scooter so she can spend an hour or so tidying up or doing whatever happens to need doing.'

'Then there's no one else in the house?'

'Not a soul.' As the words rolled off his tongue his eyes held that devilish glint she was so unnerved by. 'We're quite alone.' Then, his gaze fixed on her face, he queried, 'Does that bother you?'

Feeling trapped, her heart starting to beat in slow, heavy thuds, she denied in a stifled voice, 'No, not at all.'

'You're lying,' he said with a wolfish grin. 'You're scared out of your wits and you know it.'

Her fighting spirit aroused and determined to refute that charge of abject fear, she demanded boldly, 'Why on earth should I be scared?'

He looked as surprised as if a rabbit had turned and growled at him and, feeling a sense of triumphant satisfaction, she went on, 'So far as I'm aware, you're not a dangerous lunatic or an axe-murderer. You're a well-to-do, reputable businessman.'

If she had expected him to appear deflated, she was wrong. Instead, with a little nod of approval, he saluted her courage and agreed, 'You're pretty much right on all three counts.'

She was just congratulating herself when, a half smile hanging on his lips, he asked softly, 'And you've no other concerns? You don't think you might be in any other kind of danger?'

'I don't know what you mean,' she lied.

'It doesn't bother you that we should be here all alone with so much sexual chemistry between us?'

'I don't agree that there *is* any sexual chemistry between us.' She tried hard to sound dismissive.

'Then why do you react the way you do if I so much as touch you?'

'Because, as you're my boss, any undue familiarity makes me feel uncomfortable.'

Though aware that she sounded unbearably prim and proper, she went on, 'I wouldn't have taken the job if I hadn't been assured that you never mix business with pleasure.'

He lifted a dark brow. 'Who told you that?'

Wishing she'd kept quiet, she said hastily, 'I really don't remember.'

'Surely the only person you discussed the job with was Mrs Rogers?'

'Then it must have been her.'

'I very much doubt it.'

A shade desperately, she asked, 'Does it matter who it was?'

'You mean, so long as it's the truth?'

She squirmed under the intensity of his gaze. 'Well…yes.'

'Would it worry you if it wasn't?'

'Yes, it would.'

'Why? With a mouth like that, I can't believe you're cold, and as you told me you no longer love your ex-boyfriend, and you've no current boyfriend to consider, what is there to prevent you from having a little fun?'

'That kind of fun isn't really my style,' she informed him coolly.

'Oh?' He raised a dark brow. 'You told me you'd been on holiday with a male friend.'

Rather than admit she'd lied, she pointed out, 'That was simply a holiday and he wasn't my boss.'

'And that makes a difference?'

'I don't believe in mixing business and pleasure.'

Then, knowing it was high time she got out of there, she added with what firmness she could muster, 'I didn't get a lot of sleep last night so, if you'll excuse me, I'd like to go to bed now.'

'Of course,' he agreed with formal politeness. 'Come along and I'll see you up.'

She hadn't expected him to give in so easily and it was a moment or two before she said with equal politeness, 'Please don't trouble.'

But, following close on her heels, he assured her, 'It's no trouble at all. As a matter of fact I could do with an early night myself.'

She was climbing the spiral stairs, very conscious of how near he was, terrified that he might touch her, when he went on, 'You said you don't believe in mixing business and pleasure. Is that because you disapprove in general or because you feel it might put you in an equivocal position?'

'Both.'

'So you're not the kind of woman who thinks it's a feather in her cap to sleep with the boss?'

'No, I'm not. As far as I'm concerned, I like my working relationships to be exactly that.'

His voice soft and seductive, he said, 'What if I were to tell you that I don't regard this as just a working relationship, that I was hoping it would be a great deal more?'

'You mean you want a holiday companion?'

'You could say that.'

Emboldened by the fact that she had almost reached her room, she retorted crisply, 'In that case I would suggest you go into the nearest town and find yourself one.'

Before she could take evasive action, he had backed her against the wall and put a hand either side of her head, effectively trapping her there.

As she stared up at him, her beautiful grey eyes looking too big for her face, he asked, 'Then you don't find me in the least attractive?'

'No…' Her voice was unsteady and, afraid of what he might read into that, she added for good measure, 'You leave me cold.'

'A brave try,' he congratulated her. 'But I could soon prove the opposite. The sexual tension between us is almost palpable. If I were to kiss you now, you'd go up like dry straw.'

Knowing there was nothing for it but to brazen it out, she swallowed hard and said, 'That's where you're wrong. I'm perfectly capable of controlling *my* sexual urges.'

'You're sure about that?'

'Quite sure.'

His voice as smooth as silk, he said, 'That's a shame—I like any woman I take to bed to be eager or, at the very least, willing.'

'Well, that lets me out as I'm neither.'

He sighed. 'How very disappointing.'

Hardly daring to believe she'd won, she was bracing herself for a further onslaught when, removing his hands and taking a step back, he added, 'Oh, well, in that case, I'll say goodnight.'

Lulled into a false sense of security, she relaxed a little and answered, 'Goodnight.'

As she finished speaking, his hands moved to cup her face and lift it to his and, leaning closer, so that she could feel the sweet warmth of his breath on her lips, he murmured, 'Perhaps just a goodnight kiss to show there's no hard feelings?'

The next instant she was in his arms and his mouth was covering hers.

The shock of it ran through her entire body, tying her stomach in knots, turning her legs to jelly and bringing every nerve-ending zinging into life.

An alarm bell sounding somewhere in her brain told her she should try and stop him, make it clear that she had meant what she'd said.

But she could no more have stopped him than someone dying of thirst in a desert could have refused a life-giving drink of water.

Finding no sign of resistance, he deepened the kiss, within seconds turning her into a quivering mass of longing incapable of coherent thought.

When her slender body grew limp and pliant in his arms his kiss become passionate and coaxing, asking for—*demanding*—a response.

Lost, mindless, unable to help herself, she responded with an ardour that matched and equalled his own.

Feeling that response, he swept her up in his arms like some conqueror and, carrying her into his bedroom, set her on her feet by the four-poster bed and stripped off her dress and sandals.

Then, while she stood in her dainty underwear, he took the pins from her hair and let the dark silky mass tumble round her shoulders, before slipping the ivory satin briefs down over her slender hips and reaching behind her to unfasten her bra.

Oblivious to her surroundings, aware of nothing but him and burning with impatience, she would have helped him but her hands were shaking too much.

When he had released the clip and eased the straps off her shoulders, he tossed the delicate scrap to one side.

As he stood back to admire her beautifully shaped breasts with their dusky pink nipples, he murmured, 'Well, well, well…' Reaching out, he took the gold chain and the ring that nestled in the warm hollow between them and lifted it over her head.

Dangling it between his finger and thumb, he commented, 'A pretty bauble, and one that looks very much like an engagement ring…'

She came down to earth with a bump, every last trace of colour draining from her face to leave it paper-white, before flowing back like a crimson tide.

Oh, dear God, what was she doing? About to let another man take her to bed when she had a fiancé who loved and trusted her.

Suddenly feeling naked and vulnerable and bitterly ashamed, she snatched up the discarded dress and held it in front of her to hide her nakedness.

Swinging the chain gently so that the diamonds in the ring flashed and sparkled in the light, Zane pursued, 'Why aren't you wearing it? No, silly question. You could hardly swear that you have no ties or commitments with that on your finger.

'So who's the lucky man?'

She half shook her head.

'I think you'd better tell me.'

Though the words were softly spoken and could hardly be construed as a threat, the grim look in his green eyes made her shiver.

Her voice a mere croak, she said, 'There's no one.'

'Don't try to tell me that this little trifle came out of a Christmas cracker.'

Gathering herself, she said, 'I wasn't going to.' Then, in desperation, she lied, 'As a matter of fact, Jason gave it to me.'

'The boyfriend you broke up with six months ago?'

'Yes.'

'You didn't mention you'd been engaged.'

'As we were no longer together it didn't seem relevant.'

'Who ended things?'

'I did.'

'Why?'

She had liked Jason but she hadn't loved him and, unwilling to sleep with him, she had grown weary of his persistent attempts to persuade her into bed.

But, reluctant to tell Zane that, she answered evasively, 'It just wasn't working out.'

'But you didn't give him back his ring?' he said, the weight of the ring resting in his palm.

'No.'

'I find that strange. I had you down as the kind of woman who would. You assured me you weren't lovelorn.'

'I'm not.'

'Then why are you still wearing his ring next to your heart?'

Too late she realized that she should have allowed him to believe not only that she was still carrying a torch for Jason, but that there was some hope of them getting back together.

Taking a deep breath, she said raggedly, 'I don't think that has anything to do with you.'

'You mean it's too personal?'

'Yes.'

He laughed mirthlessly. 'I would say we're already about as up close and personal as it's possible for two people to get.

'But, before I make love to you, I would like to know *why* you're still wearing another man's ring.'

'I don't want you to make love to me. It's all been a terrible mistake. I should never have let things go this far.'

'Why did you?' he asked interestedly.

'Because I... I...'

As she floundered, he drawled, 'Don't bother to think up any lies. You "let things go this far" because you couldn't help yourself. You wanted to go to bed with me.'

Backing towards the door, she shook her head. 'I told you, it was a terrible mistake.' Then, in desperation, 'I love P—' her lips were forming the word Paul when she pulled herself up short and hastily substituted '—Jason…'

'You may be wearing *Jason's* ring—' he put the name *Jason* in quotes '—but I doubt very much if you love him. You wanted to go to bed with me.'

Knowing it was useless to keep denying it, she said, 'It would have been just sex.'

'You mean any available man would have done?'

Still backing away, she said through dry lips, 'I was missing Jason…'

Following her, he suggested silkily, 'Well, let's see what kind of substitute I make.'

'No,' she whispered. 'I can't be…'

'Unfaithful to *Jason?*' Once again he put the name in quotes. 'Yes.'

'But you can't call it being unfaithful when it's all over between you and he's been out of your life for six months.'

Trapped, knowing her only option was flight, she tried to open the door but, reaching out a hand, he held it shut.

'I want to leave,' she cried.

'Wouldn't you like this back first?' He held up the ring on its thin gold chain.

Momentarily distracted, she paused, but, instead of giving it back, he slipped the ring into the pocket of his trousers and took her wrist lightly.

'Please, Zane,' she begged shakily, 'let me go.'

'That's the first time you've called me by my Christian name,' he remarked softly.

Ignoring that, she whispered without much conviction in her voice, 'I want to leave.'

He looked down at her. 'I think you want what I want…'

Her wide eyes blinked up at him as his words held her, daring her to hear more. He murmured softly, 'I want to make long, delectable love to you, to explore that beautiful body and drive you wild with pleasure.

'I want to stroke my hands over you—your waist, your hips, your thighs, to find your hidden warmth and sweetness…'

His erotic words made her shudder even before he suited the action to the words.

'I want to bury my face against your breasts and take first one and then the other of those velvety nipples into my mouth…'

The warmth and wetness of his mouth, the slight roughness of his tongue, the delightful sensations his suckling was arousing, drove all thoughts of Paul out of her head and brought the desire she had thought dead surging back to life.

Removing the dress from her nerveless fingers, he tossed it aside. Then, lifting her in his arms, he carried her over to the bed. Held in thrall, she lay mindless, just a quivering mass of sensations, while he brought her to a fever pitch of wanting and skilfully kept her there.

She was making soft little sounds in her throat—inarticulate murmurs—before he left her for a moment to strip off his own clothes.

Naked in his turn, he stretched out beside her and with his hands and mouth resumed the exquisite torment until, unable to stand it a moment longer, she begged hoarsely, 'Oh, please, Zane…'

'Do you want me to make love to you?'

'Yes,' she whispered.

'Quite sure?'

'Yes.'

When he relented and moved over her, she welcomed his weight with pleasure, his masculine scent and warmth, the feel of his flesh against hers, the sheer *maleness* of him.

His first strong thrust caused an explosion of feeling that made her cry out and sent her tumbling and spinning into a vortex of pleasure so strong that all she could do was cling to him as though he was life itself.

Though the craving for him might have been subconscious, she had waited so many long years for this moment.

CHAPTER SEVEN

AFTER her cry, Zane had stayed quite still, his supple body poised over hers, but now he kissed her gently and began to move again, slowly, carefully, re-kindling the spark of desire she had thought, dazed and confused by the intensity of passion she'd felt when he'd entered her, could never reach more incredible heights.

His love-making was controlled and skilful—he knew how to hold back, how to wait, and he was a truly generous lover who put his partner first and gave more than he took.

And this time, though passionate, he was tender, caring, he whispered how beautiful she was, how soft and feminine, how much she delighted him.

Then, in unison, they boarded a sky-rocket to the stars and snatched a moment of supreme pleasure before drifting back to earth.

When their breathing and heart-rate returned to normal, instead of turning away, as she had half expected, he began to use his hands and mouth to take her on yet another sensual journey of pleasure.

Each time she thought she was totally sated and could feel no more, he found new ways to give her fresh delight.

At long last, when she was a limp, quivering mass of sensations, he gathered her close and, settling her so that her head was on his shoulder and his body was half supporting hers, pulled up the thin coverlet.

Almost at once, she was fast asleep.

When she awoke it was to instant and complete remembrance of everything that had happened.

There wasn't a sound apart from Zane's light, even breathing and, afraid of disturbing him, she remained quite still, hardly daring to breathe.

She was lying in the crook of his arm, her head pillowed comfortably on his shoulder. One hand was spread palm down on his bare tanned chest and she could feel the length of one hair-roughened leg against the smoothness of her own.

She couldn't see her watch but, judging by the pale light filtering through the window, it was not long after dawn.

While her entire body was as sleek and sleepily contented as a well-fed cat, her mind was wide awake and seething with a kaleidoscope of emotions.

Although Zane had given her the utmost delight, she felt sad and angry with herself, deeply ashamed of the way she had acted.

Having agreed to marry Paul and accepted his ring, how could she have behaved so wantonly, and with a man who not only didn't love her but who didn't even seem to like her?

The answer was that she had been in thrall, unable to help herself.

To him, she had been simply a woman who was there and available, a woman he scarcely knew, someone who meant less than nothing to him, while he had been part of her life for seven years, lodged in her heart and mind.

In all those long weary years since she had first met and fallen in love with him and experienced sex for the first time, she had never been tempted to sleep with any other man.

It was almost as if he had taken her over, body and soul, making it impossible for her to even consider going to bed with anyone else.

Though she had fallen for Paul, she had been secretly relieved when he had shown no sign of wanting to make love to her. But when he had eventually proposed to her, tired of being alone, wanting a home and a family, she had snatched at the chance of happiness, telling herself stoutly that when the time came everything would be all right.

However, in spite of her attempt to be confident, the doubt had lingered like a dark shadow at the back of her mind.

Until tonight.

Tonight had proved she was far from frigid and for that, at least, she should be thankful. She knew now, beyond a shadow of doubt, that she could make Paul a loving and responsive wife.

That was, if he still wanted her when she told him what had happened.

Just the thought of having to tell him tied her insides in knots, but she couldn't go into marriage with something like this on her conscience, so she would have to.

But how *could* she tell him that she'd gone to bed with Zane Lorenson?

Had it been anyone else, he might have found it in his heart to forgive her, but the mere fact that it was his hated rival would be adding insult to injury.

Though if it *had* been anyone else, she would never have succumbed in the first place. The only man in the world who could have made her react that way was Zane.

Zane, whom she had loved at first sight, with an overwhelming, life-changing love, the kind of love that could move heaven and earth.

Zane whom, in spite of the way he had treated her, she still loved and would continue to love while ever there was breath in her body.

Was it possible to love two men?

But, even as she asked herself the question, she knew with certainty that what she had felt for Paul had been mere infatuation.

She could only thank her lucky stars that her eyes had been opened in time to prevent her from marrying a man she didn't love and—after the callous way he had treated David Randall— she could no longer really like or respect.

She recognized now that the dazzling dream of a home, a family of her own and a happy-ever-after future had blinded her both to his faults and to her true feelings.

But while there was absolutely no chance of a home and a family—any kind of a future—with Zane, she could no more stop loving him than she could voluntarily stop breathing.

Which gave her no choice but to remain solitary. *One is one and all alone and ever more shall be so...*

If only their paths hadn't crossed for a second time it wouldn't have been so hard. But now, having lain with him, having experienced at least the illusion of what it would be like to be loved by him, how could she go on? How could she live the rest of her life without him?

The cold voice of reason pointed out that she had lived without him for the past seven years and, given no choice, could doubtless continue to do so.

What she couldn't—*wouldn't*—do was become his plaything, to be used and discarded as soon as the holiday was over. That would destroy her.

But, if she stayed here, she had about as much chance of holding out against him as she had of winning the lottery without buying a ticket. And while he still wanted her, he wouldn't let her go voluntarily, she was quite sure of that.

Which meant that she had to escape. Now, this minute. Before he awoke.

If only she could locate the keys and borrow the car they had driven up in. That would give her a chance to put some distance between them and it would prevent Zane from following her…

But then what could she do? Where could she go?

After a moment's thought she dismissed the idea of going to the villa where Captain Giardino was staying and asking for his help. It would be too awkward and embarrassing for all concerned.

No, she would be better off heading for the nearest airport. Though she had no euros and only a very small amount of English money, she had her credit card, which would enable her to buy petrol and a plane ticket home.

Her mind made up, she began to edge away from him inch by inch. Sleep had loosened his hold and she was able to ease herself free without disturbing him.

Slipping out of the big four-poster bed, her bare feet silent on the deep pile carpet, she gathered up her clothes and pulled them on.

She had just picked up her sandals when all at once he made a sound like a soft sigh and moved a little, making her throat go desert dry.

Rooted to the spot, she stood quite still, watching his face. The tough, sophisticated man of the world was gone. With his thick hair rumpled, his mocking eyes closed, the long lashes making dark fans on his cheeks, his jaw rough with stubble and his strong mouth relaxed in sleep, he looked boyishly handsome.

She longed to touch him, to kiss his lips one last time, but that would be madness.

Bands of iron seemed to tighten around her heart. How could she bear to leave him when, for the next two weeks at least, she could be with him, getting to know him, watching his face, listening to his voice, spending the nights in his arms…

But at what cost?

No, she *had* to go. That way she could at least keep the remnants of her pride and self-respect.

All she would have to do when she reached London was to contact his office and say she wouldn't be taking the job after all.

He need never know who she really was, or why she had applied for the position; he could get another PA and forget all about her.

Her sandals in one hand, she crossed the room and let herself out. As she closed the door, the loud click of the latch made her wince.

She had taken just a step or two when, with a nasty jolt, she remembered the ring, and Zane slipping it into the right-hand pocket of his trousers.

She couldn't leave without Paul's ring. It was worth a small fortune and, having let him down in every other way, she *had* to return that safely.

Leaving her sandals in the passageway, she crept back into the bedroom and crossed to where Zane's trousers had been tossed casually over a chair.

As she picked them up and slid her hand into the pocket, the rattle of loose change sounded loud in the stillness.

Her heart in her mouth, she glanced at him. His eyes were still closed and he showed no sign of having been disturbed.

Breathing a sigh of relief, she carefully removed the chain and ring and replaced the trousers before quietly leaving the room once more.

Picking up her sandals, she hurried along to her own room. She would have liked to stay to brush her teeth and shower and do something with her hair, but it was too big a risk.

As was packing her clothes.

Already the sun was coming up and Zane might wake at any moment.

Having tossed aside the high-heeled sandals, which would be useless to drive in, she dropped the chain and ring into her handbag, slipped into a pair of flat-heeled shoes and gathered up her jacket.

The only other things she really needed were her passport and the car keys.

Zane had put her passport into his briefcase and the last time she had seen that was when they had first arrived and he had vanished into his study carrying it.

She hadn't a clue what he'd done with the car keys. Hopefully, he would have left them either in the ignition or in his study.

If he hadn't, she would have a problem.

To say the least.

But, as being able to get away depended on having the car, somehow she would *have* to find them.

Taking the main staircase, she hastened down to the hall and opened the door of his study.

It was a big, high-ceilinged room with book-lined walls and a handsome fireplace. To one side was a well-equipped office area and, to her great relief, Zane's briefcase was lying on the desk.

It was unlocked.

Her heart beating nineteen to the dozen, she opened it and, taking out her passport, thrust it quickly into her shoulder bag.

There was no sign of the car keys, so she could only hope that they were still in the ignition.

Everywhere was quiet as she hurried across the hall and let herself out into the rear courtyard. She was attempting to close the heavy door quietly when it slipped from her fingers and shut with a bang that sounded like a thunderclap in the silence and brought her heart into her mouth.

Almost immediately, another shock rocked her. The courtyard was empty. The car was gone.

But Zane had mentioned garages, so no doubt either he or Angelo had put it away.

Making an effort to rally herself, she looked around. At the far end of the cobbled area she could see the wide doors of a pair of garages.

Suppose they were locked?

Though why would they be? No one seemed to bother locking doors in this isolated place.

The first one she reached swung up and over easily at her touch and there was the white car, its top still down.

Hurrying into the garage, which seemed a bit dim after the brightness of the courtyard, she peered into the car.

Her heart plummeted. The ignition was empty.

As she stood wondering what to do for the best, the brush of a footfall and a change in the light made her spin round.

Zane stood in the doorway.

His jaw was still rough with morning stubble and his hair was rumpled. He was wearing casual trousers and a white open-necked shirt only partially buttoned, as though he had dressed in a hurry.

But his manner was easy, laid-back as, holding up the car keys, he drawled, 'Looking for these?'

Her heart thudding against her ribs like a triphammer, she stammered, 'H-how did you…?'

'Know what you were up to?' He smiled slightly. 'I heard the latch click when you closed the bedroom door. I was just about to get up and carry you back to bed when you came back of your own accord and started to go through my trouser pockets.'

His voice caustic, he added, 'I'd always understood that that was a wife's prerogative.'

Flushing hotly, she said, 'Normally I wouldn't have done such a thing, only you'd taken my ring and I wanted it back.'

'There you have a point. And you could hardly leave without it, could you…?'

The way he spoke, almost as if he knew the truth, sent a chill through her, and she had to remind herself that her own guilty conscience was apt to make her imagine things.

'Even though you didn't stop to pack your things,' he went on sardonically, 'as you went to the trouble of retrieving your passport, I presume you *were* intending to leave, not simply to take an early morning drive?'

She made no effort to answer and after a moment he pursued, 'Just as a matter of interest, what exactly were you planning to do?'

When she remained silent, his eyes on her face, he went on, 'I presume that in the cold light of day you regretted what happened last night?'

'Yes, I did.'

'So, at a guess, you were planning to see Carlo—who not only has a chivalrous nature but speaks excellent English—and tell him I'd turned into a Big Bad Wolf—'

Flicked on the raw, she lifted her chin and cried angrily, 'I was going to do no such thing!'

'No?'

'No!'

'Why not?'

'Because it wouldn't have been true. You…' Her voice shook so much she was forced to stop. But after a moment she went on bravely, 'You didn't force yourself on me.'

'Thank you… But you *were* planning to appeal to him for help?'

'I most certainly wasn't! It would have been far too awkward and embarrassing for everyone concerned.'

His glance holding a touch of respect, he asked, 'So what *were* you going to do?'

'I was hoping to drive to the nearest airport and get a plane back to London.'

'Dear me, homesick already?' he mocked. 'And I thought you wanted to come to Tuscany.'

Through gritted teeth, she said, 'I didn't want to come to Tuscany. As a matter of fact, I didn't want to go *anywhere* with you.'

He pounced. 'But you knew perfectly well there was travelling involved before you took the job.'

Having no answer to that, she said defensively, 'I should never have taken it. This whole thing has been a mistake from the start and I want to leave.'

'Why? It can't be the job itself. We haven't even started work yet. And you were honest enough to admit that last night I didn't force myself on you.

'In fact, if you're being *totally* honest, you'll admit that you wanted me just as much as I wanted you…'

She longed to shake his certainty, to swear she hadn't, but no matter how she tried she couldn't bring herself to frame the lie.

'That being so,' he went on, 'I think you should reconsider. After all, we haven't even been here a full day yet. You've given yourself no time to adjust.

'And if you really don't want to share my bed, all you have to do is say *no,* and mean it. When it comes to personal matters, it's your decision.'

She was just assimilating that when he added wickedly, 'Though if I don't agree with that decision, I reserve the right to try a little friendly persuasion.'

The devilish gleam in his eye and the crooked smile that put grooves beside his mouth made him practically irresistible.

She was shaken to the core by the temptation to stay, to have just a few more days in his company. But if she stayed she couldn't trust herself to say no and mean it, so for the sake of her pride she *had* to go.

Though was she making a big mistake in putting her pride first? He was the only man in the world for her and she wanted to be in his bed, in his arms, feel his naked flesh next to hers, enjoy the weight of his body, revel in his maleness.

This would be her only chance to snatch a little, all too brief, happiness.

But could she be happy, knowing that to him it would be just a casual exchange of pleasure, while to her it would be mortgaging her soul?

How could she bear the pain of meaning nothing to him while he meant everything to her? And when this 'holiday' was over and he'd had his fun, she would be left alone and desolate.

'I don't want time to adjust,' she told him sharply. 'I'm going back to London.'

He shook his head. 'I think not. At least not until I'm ready to take you.'

'You can't keep me here against my will.'

'Want to bet?' he asked laconically, and watched her beautiful grey eyes widen.

'Now, can I suggest that we go back inside and act like civilized people?'

'Your behaviour is anything but civilized,' she cried jerkily. 'If you were half civilized you wouldn't be keeping me a prisoner.'

He smiled as if genuinely amused. 'You do have an overdeveloped sense of the melodramatic.'

'Well, what else would you call it?'

'Hardly "keeping you a prisoner". If you're looking forward to the excitement of being chained up in a dungeon, I'm afraid you're going to be sadly disappointed. I was thinking rather more mundanely of having some coffee and a shower before breakfast.'

Although the thought of a coffee and a shower was extremely tempting, reluctant to give in and go back with him, she hesitated.

But what was the use of continuing to resist? Where would it get her? There was no way she could win. He was so much stronger than she was, both physically and when it came to will-power.

As, with an inward sigh, she gave in and turned to accompany him, she heard his soft laugh and guessed he had been following her train of thought with his usual deadly accuracy.

Swinging the garage door into place, he put a proprietorial arm round her waist.

Angered by his amusement, his ability to walk in and out of her mind, and even more by the casual arrogance of his touch, she made an attempt to pull free but he wouldn't allow it.

Recognizing that he'd thrown down the gauntlet and knowing she was in no position to pick it up, she stared at him stonily.

Looking at her set face, he said, 'On second thoughts, as I hate to disappoint a lady, if you're fancying a spot of melodrama, here goes…'

He gave a villainous laugh and declaimed, 'Ha ha, me proud beauty, at last I have you in my clutches to do with as I will!'

She was surprised into laughter by his clowning. Laughter that instantly relieved the tension and lightened the mood.

'That's better,' he said with satisfaction. 'Now, shall we go and have that coffee?'

Her resistance temporarily at an end, she allowed him to shepherd her into the house and up the stairs she had crept down only a short time ago.

One flight up, he led her along a wide corridor and through a doorway into an attractively furnished morning room with French windows that opened on to a sunny terrace.

While he switched on the coffee-making machine and produced cups, installed in one of the armchairs, Gail made an effort to order her thoughts. But it was like trying to order motes dancing in the air and she gave up.

As the machine hummed and the appetising smell of coffee began to fill her nostrils, she watched him, letting her thoughts drift.

If the keys had been in the car she would have been gone by now, out of his life, this little episode finished. Over.

But, though it had been traumatic in a lot of ways, part of her hadn't wanted it to end, and that part was treacherously happy to be still here, to be near him, to be able to just watch him.

All his movements had an easy, coordinated grace and he was beautiful, with a wholly masculine beauty. It was a pleasure to be able to sit and feast her eyes on him while he was occupied and totally unaware of her scrutiny.

He glanced up suddenly and, afraid of what he might read in her eyes, she looked hastily away.

Carrying the tray over, he set it down on a small oblong table and handed her a cup before taking his seat opposite her.

While they drank their coffee, which was hot and strong and fragrant, Gail avoided looking at him. But all the time she was aware that he studied her contemplatively as though, having kept her here against her will, he was wondering how to play it.

Though *why* had he kept her here? It wasn't the way any ordinary businessman would treat an employee who insisted on leaving.

But then nothing about their brief association had been ordinary.

And surely it wasn't simply because he wanted her in his bed when, with his looks and charisma—not to mention his money—he would have no trouble finding plenty of willing, not to say eager, women...

He broke into her thoughts to ask politely, 'Would you like any more coffee?'

Shaking her head, she answered with equal politeness, 'No, thank you.'

He rose and, having put their empty cups on the tray, took both her hands and pulled her to her feet, before handing her her bag and jacket. 'Then let's go and have that shower.'

They climbed the spiral staircase up to the next floor without speaking but, when he would have taken her into the master bedroom, she dug her heels in and protested, 'I don't know what you've got in mind, but if you think—'

His voice innocent, he said, 'I thought we'd agreed on a shower?'

'This is *your* room.'

'It's *our* room,' he corrected her.

Our room... Her heart gave a little lurch.

Taking a deep breath and holding tightly to her resolve not to become just a holiday plaything, she said as evenly as possible, 'A short while ago you told me that when it comes to personal matters it's my decision.'

'That's right. So?'

'So I don't want to share your room. Or your bed. I don't want to stay here at all.'

Those clear, dark green eyes smiled into hers. Then, brushing back her long fall of dark hair and nuzzling his bristly face against the side of her neck, he reminded her, 'But I also said that if I don't agree with that decision I reserve the right to try and change your mind.'

'You're wasting your time; I won't change my...' She

faltered to a halt, distracted by the way his mouth was exploring the tender juncture where neck met shoulder.

Ignoring her half formed protest, he suggested, 'Suppose we start by sharing a shower?'

'I don't want to share a shower,' she croaked.

'Why not?' He nibbled his way back to her ear, making shivers run up and down her spine. 'It can be quite exhilarating. We'll soap each other and see who has the most fun.'

Trying to ignore a *frisson* of heated excitement that ran along her nerve-endings, she said severely, 'I didn't come here to have fun. I came to work.'

His lips following the pure line of her jaw, he murmured, 'Why so eager to start work? This is a holiday first and foremost.'

Planting soft baby kisses on her cheeks and temples, her closed eyelids, he coaxed, 'Try letting your hair down. You have no ties, no man in your life…'

Now she had realized that she'd never really loved Paul and had decided to give him back his ring, that was true as far as it went.

But while he *thought* she was his fiancée, *thought* she was still loyal to him, how could she betray him further by deliberately involving herself with a man he hated?

The answer was that she couldn't.

But Zane was going on softly, 'And, beneath that air of unworldly innocence, you're a responsive, passionate woman who's a delight to make love to. A woman who needs a man…'

Clinging to her principles like someone drowning clung to a straw, she said desperately, 'I'm not the kind to have affairs, or to sleep with the boss. I don't want to lose my pride, my self-respect…'

'You gave them into my keeping when you slept in my bed last night,' Zane said, dropping a kiss at the corner of her mouth, 'so I can't see you've anything to lose.'

He was right, of course. If she'd valued her pride and self-respect all that much, she wouldn't have acted as she had.

But somehow, the fact that he had said '*you gave them into my keeping*', rather than *you lost them* made all the difference.

He felt the tension, the resistance, drain away and, as he continued with those teasing kisses, he whispered, 'Will it really be such a hardship to stay? To share my room and my bed?'

It would be no hardship at all. Even though he didn't love her, it would mean being as close to heaven as she was ever likely to be while she was still on earth.

But even that thought was lost as he finally claimed her mouth and deepened the kiss.

When he finally lifted his head and led her through to his bathroom she went willingly, anticipation making her heart beat like a drum and turning the blood running through her veins into molten lava.

Turning on the shower, he quickly stripped off first her clothes and then his own and, taking her hand, stepped beneath the flow of water.

Indicating a bottle of shower gel, he said teasingly, 'Your turn first.'

Hoping he would put her rising colour down to the warmth of the water, she squeezed the pine-scented gel into her palms.

His dark hair flattened seal-like to his head, water running down his face and muscular body, he stood there at his ease, giving her no help.

Keeping her eyes firmly fixed on the tanned column of his throat, she began to smooth the gel over his broad, glistening shoulders and chest, his ribcage and his lean waist.

When she came to his flat belly, she hesitated.

She heard his soft laugh before he said mockingly, 'If you feel a maidenly reluctance to go any further, I'll quite understand.'

Blushing furiously now, but at the same time longing to look at him, to touch him, she made an effort to shrug off her inhibitions.

Though their relationship was fated to be just a short one, why allow false modesty to stand in her way? He was her one and only love. The only man she had ever wanted. The only man she *would* ever want.

Lowering her gaze for the first time and glorying in his sheer maleness, she proved that any maidenly reluctance she might have felt had, temporarily at least, vanished.

Her light touch had a powerful effect and after a moment or two he caught her wrists and, holding her hands away from him, told her huskily, 'My turn now.'

Daring, for the first time, to tease him, she said, 'Can't take it, huh?'

Surprised into laugher in his turn, he said, 'Sassy, eh?'

Releasing her hands, he bent to lick drops of water from her pink nipples before soaping her slender body with a thoroughness that made every nerve-ending zing into life and sent her pulses racing madly.

Then, lifting her, his hands cupping her buttocks, he said in her ear, 'Put your arms round my neck and wrap your legs round me…'

CHAPTER EIGHT

WHILE the water cascaded down and the scented steam rose around them, he made long, delectable love to her, leaving her limp and quivering with pleasure.

As soon as their breathing and heart rate had returned to normal he switched off the water and, handing her out, wrapped her in a fluffy bath sheet before rubbing first her dripping hair and then, more cursorily, his own.

When, a towel draped around his lean hips, he had leisurely dried and kissed every inch of her, he helped her into a white towelling bathrobe and tied the belt around her slender waist.

Rather than regretting what she'd done, she was floating on cloud nine, and she could only be glad that she had chosen to ignore her pride and follow her heart.

An ardent and passionate lover, he had treated her as though she was precious to him, making it hard to believe that in reality he didn't care, that she meant less than nothing to him.

In fact his tenderness towards her had given her hope that it was more than just sex, that he might come to care.

They seemed to be on the same wavelength, share a closeness. Several times she had turned to look at him, only to find him turning to look at her at the very same moment.

The robe was one of his and it swamped her, coming down

almost to her ankles, the sleeves hanging over her hands, yet it felt right and she was happy wearing it.

As, her hair in a damp tangle around her shoulders, she began to roll up the sleeves, he smiled and suggested, 'There's plenty of space left in the wardrobe and the drawers, so don't you think it might be a good idea to transfer your belongings?'

She nodded and, the small commitment made, felt a thrill of excited happiness. *Our room...*

Her reward was a kiss and then, as if he couldn't get enough of her, another. 'In that case, if you'd like to go and get organized while I brush my teeth and shave...?'

When she had picked up her discarded clothes and put them in the laundry basket, she reluctantly went.

Loving him as she did, every second in his company, every new thing, was precious to her, and if she hadn't been afraid of what he might read into it, she would have lingered to watch him shave.

Telling herself that she was behaving like some lovesick adolescent rather than a twenty-four-year-old businesswoman, she cleaned her teeth and brushed her hair, before dressing in a summery skirt and top and pulling on a pair of sandals.

Leaving her face innocent of make-up and her dark hair loose around her shoulders, she gathered together her belongings and put them in neat piles on the un-slept-in bed.

When she started to transfer them to the big airy bedroom next door, she found both that and the bathroom were empty. Zane was obviously downstairs preparing breakfast.

As he had said, there was plenty of space in the walk-in wardrobe and the tall chest of drawers and it didn't take long to put everything neatly away. That done, she made her way downstairs to find him.

As she had surmised, he was in the kitchen, which lay

between the dining room and the morning room. Wearing smart casual trousers and a silk open-necked shirt, a tea towel draped around his lean hips, he was turning sizzling bacon in a pan.

Glancing up, he invited, 'Come here.'

She went obediently.

He tilted her face with his free hand and studied her for a moment, before telling her, 'You're the only woman I know who can look even more beautiful and sexy with no make-up and a shiny nose.'

Bending his dark head, he kissed her mouth—a lingering kiss, a lover's kiss, that made her heart lurch drunkenly and opened up a Pandora's box of hopes and dreams.

If only he loved her, if only they were a real couple, sharing a real holiday...

But, recalling what his ex-PA had said about women having no real place in his life, she knew it was useless to hope that he might ever come to care for her.

Yet, even while she admitted that it was like crying for the moon because she wanted it so very much, she couldn't kill that faint hope.

And, no matter what, she had to be thankful that, for the next couple of weeks, she had the chance to be with him, to spend the days in his company and the nights in his arms...

Transferring his attention back to the pan, he said, 'Help yourself to some juice... I trust you like bacon and eggs?'

Taking a glass of freshly squeezed orange juice, she answered lightly, 'Who doesn't? Though at home I usually only have toast and coffee.'

'Well, as this kind of holiday can be...shall we say... strenuous...you might need to keep your strength up.'

Feeling herself start to blush, she looked around the vast farmhouse kitchen while she sipped the cool, tangy juice.

The decor was off-white and burnt ochre and the floor was

made of wide planks of softly glowing wood. Two massive dressers displaying colourful pottery flanked a farmhouse table.

Set between long windows was a wood-burning range and, in front of it, a low sturdy coffee table and a couple of comfortable-looking armchairs stood on a hand-crafted rug.

An electric cooker, a fridge-freezer and all mod cons had been cleverly blended in without detracting from its overall rustic appeal.

'Like it?' he queried.

'Yes, I do. It's attractive and homely. Absolutely perfect for this place.'

'I'm glad you think so. Apart from the fact that it wouldn't have fitted in, I don't really care for the purely-functional-glass-and-chrome-type kitchens.

'If I'm on my own and the weather isn't too good, I often eat in here.'

Taking the dishes of crisp bacon and scrambled eggs, he added, 'But today, as it's so beautiful and sunny, I suggest we eat on the morning room terrace.'

Sitting in the sun, they ate a leisurely breakfast and were at the coffee stage before Zane broke the companionable silence to ask, 'What would you like to do today?'

'I really don't mind. I'm happy to do anything you want to do.'

'What if we have a relaxing hour by the pool, then go to Florence for lunch and spend the rest of the afternoon sight-seeing?'

'If we have an hour by the pool, can we get to Florence in time for lunch?'

'We can if we go by helicopter. I have one at the airfield. It's useful for shorter hops and being able to land almost anywhere makes it ideal.'

Of course. She still hadn't totally caught up with the fact that he was a wealthy man who had the means to order his life exactly how he wanted it.

'So what do you think?'

'It sounds just perfect.'

Smiling at her enthusiasm, he got up and, taking her hands, pulled her to her feet. 'Then let's make a start by having that swim.'

'I'd love to, but I haven't got a costume.'

'That isn't a problem; we can go skinny-dipping. The pool area isn't directly overlooked, so unless someone came down specially…'

Amused by her horrified expression, he added, 'Of course, if you really don't like the idea I'm sure I could dig out a costume for you.'

Breathing a sigh of relief, she said gratefully, 'If you could…'

Hand in hand, they made their way downstairs and across the hall. As they reached the rear courtyard they heard the buzz of a motor scooter approaching and a moment later Angelo appeared with his mother on the pillion seat.

Dismounting nimbly, Maria gave them both a beaming smile. '*Buon giorno*, Signor Lorenson… Signorina…'

Returning the smile, Gail said, '*Buon giorno.*'

'*Buon giorno,*' Zane followed suit and crossed to have a few words with the housekeeper before rejoining Gail and escorting her to a flight of stone steps that curved down the hillside.

When they reached the bottom, she saw that the pool was large, almost Olympic size, and its blue waters looked extremely inviting.

As he had said, the pool area was surrounded by trees and shrubs and was pleasantly secluded. A scattering of sunbeds and loungers were interspersed with umbrella-shaded tables.

At one side, next to a vine-covered arbour, there were two

small white changing cabins which, he told her, had been erected mainly for the convenience of any possible visitors.

He led her into the nearest one, which had a bench running round it, a storage area for clothes, a long cupboard with a mirror and a shower cubicle.

Having rummaged about in the cupboard, which was stacked with towels, towelling robes and various toiletries, he produced a black one-piece swimsuit and a bright yellow bikini.

Putting them on the bench, he said casually, 'Andrea's about your size, so either of these should fit.' Dropping a light kiss on her mouth, he went to get changed.

Andrea... Presumably one of the women he had brought here previously. Gail experienced a swift, painful pang of jealousy.

Though what was the point of being jealous of a woman who presumably belonged in the past? Where, if he ran true to form, in a couple of weeks' time she too would belong.

The depressing thought enveloped her like a dark cloud shutting out the sun.

But if she only had a couple of weeks, what was the point of wasting them being miserable?

As she made an effort to recapture her earlier, more optimistic mood, her old school motto sprang into her mind. *Carpe diem...* Seize the day.

Yes, better by far to try and be happy and enjoy each day to the full than worry about the future.

Running an eye over the costumes Zane had produced, she immediately discarded the minuscule bikini in favour of the more modest black one-piece.

Only when she had it on she discovered that, cut high at the thighs and low at the back and the bust, it wasn't modest at all.

Staring at herself in the mirror, she almost gasped. Though for some years she had regarded her figure as quite reasonable, in the designer swimsuit it was spectacular—the style emphasising her slim waist, the curve of her hips, her generous bust and long slender legs.

Was this how Zane had seen her when he'd described her as beautiful?

Feeling shy, in spite of all that had happened, she ventured forth to find that a couple of towelling robes had been tossed over a chair and he was already in the pool.

Wearing black trunks, he was cleaving the water in a leisurely, graceful crawl without a splash and hardly seeming to breathe.

She stood watching him until, about to make a turn, he spotted her and heaved himself out.

Water streaming from him, he stood and stared at her, then said huskily, 'If by any chance you've changed your mind about having a swim, I can think of something better to do.'

Though very much tempted, she managed to say, 'No, I haven't changed my mind.'

Grinning at her prim tone, he said, 'Pity… Come on, then, I'll race you to the other end and back. The winner can claim a kiss.'

'I'm out of practice.'

'I'll give you a start.'

Very conscious that he was watching, she dived in and, knowing that it had been a good, clean dive, set off at a fast racing crawl.

Though, during her last year at school she had represented her house at all the swimming galas, she hadn't swum for years and knew quite well that, even giving her a start, he could easily beat her.

Still, she was determined to give him a run for his money and was halfway down the pool when he caught up and kept pace with her.

They turned in unison and set off back.

She touched first.

Surfacing by her side, he stood up and shook the water out of his eyes, then gravely offered her his pursed lips.

She was forced to stifle a laugh before saying accusingly, 'You let me win.'

'Does it really matter who kisses who?' he asked.

'Suppose I don't want to claim a kiss?'

Pulling her close, he threatened, 'If you don't collect your winnings I shall be forced to declare the race null and void and insist on a rerun.'

'Oh, well, in that case…'

She stood on tiptoe to kiss him. He had just deepened the kiss when the sharp click of approaching footsteps made them both look up.

Walking towards them was a stunning blonde with a model-girl figure, wearing high heels and a silk designer suit patterned in peacock shades of blue and green and purple.

Judging by her expression, she had seen what had taken place. But, quickly masking the look of jealous anger, she smiled at Zane and called, '*Caio, caro.*'

His face impassive, he answered, '*Caio,* Andrea.'

So this beautiful woman, who reminded her sharply of Rona, was Andrea.

Heaving himself out of the water, Zane turned to offer Gail his hands.

But, feeling a tightness round her heart and a hollow emptiness in the pit of her stomach, she had turned away and was swimming towards the steps.

By the time she reached them, he was waiting to help her out.

As he straightened, the blonde threw her arms around his neck and, pressing herself against him, kissed him full on the lips before bursting into a flood of Italian.

'Careful—' unwinding her arms, he held her away a little '—you'll get saturated…'

Making a little moue, she took a step back and said something, to which Zane answered, 'Not at all,' before holding out one of the towelling robes for Gail to put on and shrugging into his own.

Then, formally, he introduced the two women. 'Gail, this is Signorina Lombardi…'

'How do you do?' Gail murmured, pleased that her voice was steady.

At close quarters, she could see that Andrea was much younger than she had first appeared—at a guess, no more than eighteen or nineteen. But she had a veneer of glamour and sophistication that made her seem considerably older.

'Andrea, I'd like you to meet Miss North.'

'*Piacere,*' Andrea said, her perfectly made-up face cold and set. '*Lei parla Italiano?*'

'No, Gail doesn't speak Italian,' Zane told her, 'so perhaps you'd be kind enough to speak English?'

Her full red lips pouting, she made what was clearly a protest.

Unmoved, Zane retorted, 'You speak excellent English, as I'm quite sure you know.'

'Oh, very well,' she agreed sulkily. 'In order to please you I'll do as you ask.'

'Good girl.'

'Though I still don't find it easy to express myself fully in English.'

He looked about to say, *Rubbish!* Instead he pointed out mildly, 'Then this will be good practice.'

Running a scarlet-tipped finger down the side of his cheek, she accused, 'You're being cruel to me.'

'Not at all.'

Giving up, she observed, 'I presume Miss North is your new PA, no?' Her dark eyes sweeping Gail from head to toe, she added with saccharine sweetness, 'I see my swimsuit fits her.'

As the colour rose in Gail's cheeks, Zane said repressively, 'Miss North had omitted to pack a costume, so *I* suggested she borrow one of yours.'

'I'm sure she thinks it very noble of you to take the blame.'

'Don't be catty, Andrea,' he said, as though she were a child. Then, blandly, 'Don't forget you have a bikini here if you'd like to join us for a swim.'

She shuddered. 'You know perfectly well that I never go in the water, *caro*. As far as I'm concerned, pools are for sitting by.'

'This one was intended for healthy exercise, not just a display of physical charms.'

'You're being cruel again.'

When he said nothing, with a provocative smile, she went on, 'But even if you do enjoy being cruel to me, it's very nice that you're here. I've missed you so much, *caro*...'

Feeling *de trop*, Gail murmured, 'If you'll excuse me,' and began to move away.

His fingers closing round her upper arm, keeping her where she was, Zane drawled, 'There's really no need to rush off.'

'I'd like to go and get changed.'

'Let her go if she wants to,' Andrea said.

'It's what *I* want that counts,' he informed her coolly, 'and I happen to want Miss North to stay.'

Reining in her anger, Andrea shrugged her slim shoulders. 'As you wish. Though I would have much preferred to be able to talk in private, without an *employee* being present.'

As his mouth tightened, she hastily changed the subject. 'You are really very naughty; you didn't say a word about coming to Severo...'

'No,' he agreed calmly and, steering Gail to the nearest lounger, pressed her into it, totally ignoring the pleading look she gave him.

Giving all her attention to Zane and ignoring Gail completely, Andrea chose an umbrella-shaded lounger and, crossing her shapely silk-clad legs, persisted, '*Why* didn't you let me know you were coming?'

'Firstly, it was all rather sudden and, secondly, I understood that you were bored with Montecino and had gone back to Rome and taken Moira with you.'

'Yes, she's staying at my apartment so we can shop together. Rome has all the best shops, and time is getting short.'

Patting the lounger next to hers, she invited, 'Why don't you sit beside me for a while, *caro?*'

He sat down, but in the empty lounger between the two women, rather than the one she had indicated.

For a split second Andrea appeared put out. Then, giving him a little girl look, she asked plaintively, 'You *are* pleased to see me, aren't you?'

His face softening and his tone becoming indulgent, he answered, 'Of course.'

Then, casually, 'How did you know I was here?'

'When I talked to Paolo yesterday he mentioned that you had just flown in, but he warned me that it was to be a working holiday. Still, I couldn't miss the chance to see you, so I decided on a flying visit and caught the evening plane. Paolo loaned me a car so I could come over to see you.

'Unfortunately, I cannot stay long. He wants me to go to Pianosa with him. There is a villa there that he is thinking of buying…

'Though I love my brother dearly, I am not looking forward to the journey. He likes to keep the top down and the sun is bad for my skin. Just driving here it was so hot—'

'Then I'll go and rustle up some refreshments,' Zane broke smoothly into the flow.

As he started to rise, she stopped him. 'There is no need. When your housekeeper said you were by the pool, I told her to bring some cool drinks down…'

At that moment Maria appeared, carrying a tray which she placed on one of the low tables.

'*Grazie,* Maria,' Zane said.

She gave an unsmiling nod and departed, her back ramrod straight.

It appeared that something, or *someone,* had ruffled her composure.

'I don't know how you can stand that surly, arrogant creature,' Andrea complained as Zane helped both women to a tall frosted glass of fruit juice. 'Couldn't you get somebody more…'

'Servile?' he suggested when she hesitated.

'Someone who knows her place,' Andrea finished defiantly. 'She was barely civil to me.'

'Whereas you were perfectly polite to her?'

'Why should I be polite to paid servants?'

Once again Gail found herself thinking how very alike Andrea and Rona were, both in appearance and character. It seemed that Zane attracted, and was attracted by, that type of woman.

Now he was saying, again with that air of indulgence, 'My dear Andrea, when you marry and become the mistress of a house, if you want to keep any staff you'll need to change your attitude.'

'Don't be silly, *caro,*' she retorted airily. 'One can always keep servants so long as there is money to pay their wages…'

With a slight shrug, he let it go.

Brushing back the long, straight fall of gleaming blonde

hair, she complained, 'I've hardly seen you in the past few months, and when I talk to you on the phone you tell me so little. I never really know what you do with yourself when you are alone in London.'

'I work,' he said laconically.

'How boring.'

'While you, I imagine, have been nearly bankrupting your papa.'

'Papa has plenty of money,' she said dismissively, 'and, as I am his only daughter, he wants me to look my best for the wedding.

'Moira and I have been out almost every day, shopping for a trousseau or being fitted for our dresses. Rocco, who has designed all the dresses, says they will look absolutely beautiful, so I hope you will like mine.'

'I'm sure I will.'

She covered his hand with hers. 'Though the wedding is only a month away, it seems a long time before we can be together in church, and I confess I am impatient for the happy day…'

Sitting silently listening, Gail felt as if she had been mortally wounded and was slowly bleeding to death inside.

Zane was going to marry Andrea Lombardi, who was so like Rona. Rona, whom he had once loved.

His ex-PA had said that he had no real place in his life for a woman, but she had been wrong.

No wonder Andrea had been angry and jealous when, with the wedding only a month away, she had seen another woman kissing her future husband.

In the circumstances she had been very restrained. She could well have kicked up a fuss.

But perhaps, as they had been apart and well aware that he was a red-blooded man, she had half-expected him to be having a last fling before the wedding?

Though, knowing he was committed to Andrea, how could he have made love to *her* in the way he had?

The answer was that he couldn't unless he was completely unscrupulous, and she didn't want to believe that.

Even after what had happened that evening more than seven years ago, she had always considered him to be an honourable man.

Yet, thinking about the way he had kept her here against her will, how he had used the chemistry between them to make her want to stay, it seemed he really had no scruples…

Her painful thoughts were interrupted by Andrea getting to her feet and saying wistfully, 'It will be almost a month before I see you again, and I will miss you so much, *caro*…'

'When you get back to Rome you'll be far too busy shopping to give me a thought.'

'How can you say that?'

'Quite easily.'

'You know I am wild about you.' Throwing her arms around his neck, she gave him a lingering kiss, which he appeared rather to endure than return.

A reluctant spectator, Gail found herself wondering how he could be so offhand with his future wife.

Unless he didn't really love her.

But, if he didn't love her, why was he marrying her?

Perhaps he wanted a family, a mother for his children, someone to leave his money to?

Though why Andrea? Admittedly she was beautiful, but then so were a lot of other women. Perhaps he had chosen her simply because she reminded him of Rona—a woman he had wanted and been unable to keep…?

Having freed himself from Andrea's embrace, Zane said crisply, 'You'd better be starting back or Paolo won't have time to get over to Pianosa.'

When she looked crestfallen at his dismissal, he added more kindly, 'Come on, I'll walk back to the car with you and see you off.'

Turning to Gail, he suggested, 'If you'd like to shower and dress, either here or up at the house, I'll be with you shortly.'

Wondering if he intended to go on with their plans as if nothing had happened, she found her voice and queried through stiff lips, 'Are you still thinking of going to Florence?'

Sounding surprised that she should need to ask, he said, 'Of course…'

It was the answer she had hoped for. Going to Florence made it so much easier to put into practice the decision she had just made.

She was turning away when he added, 'I'll give the airfield a ring and ask them to have the chopper standing by.'

Looking anything but pleased, Andrea slipped a hand through his arm and leaned in close.

As the pair disappeared up the steps Gail could hear the other woman talking volubly. She was speaking Italian now but, judging by her tone, she was railing against something or someone.

Probably herself, Gail reflected bitterly.

Though, in all honesty, she couldn't blame her. Had she been in Andrea's place, *she* would have felt anger and resentment.

Who wouldn't?

Quickly she showered and dried herself, while thoughts tumbled through her head like sad clowns.

As she began to pull on her clothes, the question she had already asked herself came back to torment her—when Zane was engaged to be married, how *could* he have acted in the way he had?

But that was a case of the pot calling the kettle black, she realized with shame. When she had gone to bed with him, *she* had been engaged to another man.

So it wasn't all Zane's fault and, though he might have tried to deceive Andrea, she couldn't say he had deceived *her*. He had made no promises, no commitment of any kind, had told her no lies and offered her nothing beyond pleasure and physical gratification.

And, while she had been unable to douse a small glimmer of hope that something more lasting might come of it, she had known and come to terms with the fact that, as far as he was concerned, their relationship was intended to be merely a brief holiday fling.

However, knowing that he belonged to another woman changed everything. She *couldn't* and *wouldn't* come to terms with that.

Though she didn't like Andrea, she couldn't help but feel sorry for her. She knew what it was like to be madly in love with a man who didn't care a jot about her.

Therefore it was imperative that she should go, and as soon as possible. But if she told him to his face that she thought he was acting like a swine and that she intended to go back to London, he might still try to prevent her from leaving.

Supposing he did, even knowing the truth she couldn't trust herself to remain in control of her emotions, and if she let him so much as suspect that she was in love with him it would be handing him a weapon he would certainly use against her.

So, once they were in Florence, she must find an opportunity to slip away. It would mean leaving all her things at the villa, but so long as she had her passport with her she could manage.

All she would need was enough money to take either a bus or a taxi to the airport…

Like most men, Zane carried loose change in his trouser

pockets and almost certainly a notecase in his jacket. All she had to do was borrow what she thought she might need.

Remembering Andrea's passionate embrace, she guessed that the leave-taking would be a protracted affair, so now was probably the best time to do what she had to.

Draping the damp swimming things over a rail, she hastened back to the house and up to the bedroom they had been sharing.

There was no sign of Zane and, having checked that the bathroom was empty, she looked round for the most likely jacket.

Hanging over the back of a chair was the one he had worn at the airport.

She hurried over and, her hands shaking, felt in the inner pocket. Yes! There was a wallet with a sizeable wad of euros.

Peeling off several notes, she thrust them hurriedly into her bag. That should be enough for the taxi fare and any possible airport departure tax.

Her hands still unsteady, she brushed and coiled her hair and applied a touch of make-up. She had just gathered up her bag and jacket when the door opened and Zane came in, showered and dressed, his damp hair neatly combed.

Smiling at her, he observed, 'All ready, I see.'

Common sense told her that if she didn't want him to suspect anything she would have to make an effort to act normally, but her whole face felt stiff and, try as she might, she was unable to return his smile.

He gave her a searching look and a combination of guilt and anger made her heart start to thud so loudly she thought he must surely hear.

But, making no comment, he picked up his jacket and, a hand at her waist, said, 'Let's go.'

CHAPTER NINE

THE drive down the hill and along the valley floor was made without a word being spoken. Gail could think of nothing to say, and Zane seemed to be sunk in thought.

At the airfield the silver helicopter was waiting, its rotor blades whirring gently, its paintwork gleaming in the sun.

A small group of engineers and ground staff were standing by chatting, but there was no sign of Captain Giardino and it soon became apparent that Zane was going to pilot the helicopter himself.

When she was settled in the passenger seat, he slid in alongside and, turning to look at her, asked, 'Your first flight?'

She nodded.

'How do you feel about it?'

'Fine,' she managed.

Clear green eyes looked searchingly into cloudy grey. 'You seem very tense and uptight.'

'I'm quite all right, really I am. How far away is Florence airport?'

'We're not going to the airport. We'll be landing at the Firenze Boscolo Hotel.

'Look, if you're nervous, we can always cancel today's trip and go to Florence another day by road.'

The thought of the possible consequences of having to spend another night under his roof was enough to spur her on.

'I'm not nervous,' she denied quickly, 'and I can't wait to see Florence.' But she was aware that her voice wasn't quite steady and he didn't believe her.

'Well, if you like we could go by road now and stop for a meal en route, but it wouldn't leave much time for sightseeing.'

She might well have chosen that option if she hadn't been so desperate to get to Florence quickly and make her escape. As it was…

'I'm quite happy to fly,' she told him firmly.

'That's good.' He leaned forward to kiss her.

Instinctively she flinched.

Taking her chin, he tilted her face and studied it. 'What's wrong?' he enquired coolly.

'Nothing,' she whispered.

'In that case…' As if making a point, he kissed her with slow deliberation.

When he lifted his head, haunted by the way Andrea had kissed him, she wiped the back of her hand across her mouth.

His jaw tightened as he noticed that telling gesture but he made no comment and, reaching for a set of headphones, gave his full attention to the task in hand.

Their lift-off into the blue sky, though noisy, seemed effortless and soon the airfield was spread beneath them like a scale model.

Fascinated by the novelty of it, she soon found that flying over the sunlit Tuscan countryside was a fascinating experience and one that, had the circumstances been different, she would have thoroughly enjoyed.

Though Zane glanced at her from time to time, he made no effort to talk until, after twenty minutes or so, the countryside began to give way to outlying streets and buildings and Gail found they were approaching a built-up area.

'Won't be long now,' he said above the noise. 'Just coming into view is the River Arno, which runs through Florence…'

She had no trouble locating the broad brown sash of water and as they approached the centre of the city she saw that at this point the river was spanned by several bridges.

'In a moment,' he went on, 'you should get a good view of the Ponte Vecchio.'

In spite of all her woes and anxieties, it was a thrill to see that famous medieval bridge, with its spectacular line of small shops and houses running down either side.

Supported on brackets that overhung the river, they were painted in mellow shades of yellow and, with their wooden shutters, wrought ironwork and awnings, had kept their medieval appearance.

Seen from the air, Florence was absolutely breathtaking, with its imposing squares and magnificent architecture, its tall campaniles and domed churches, its narrow, canyon-like streets and fascinating jumble of rooftops.

By the time they came in to land in the grounds of the Hotel Firenze Boscolo, Gail's earlier sombre mood had changed to one of reckless abandonment.

Zane might have feet of clay, but she would continue to love him while ever there was breath in her body, so she would stop worrying and enjoy to the utmost the short time they would spend together in this wonderful city.

When he had stopped the engine and removed his headset, he turned to her and in the sudden relative quietness queried politely, 'Not too bad an ordeal, I hope?'

She was able to say with truth, 'No, I enjoyed it.'

'That's good.'

She waited for his kiss, but this time he made no attempt to kiss her and she was disappointed.

As the rotor blades stopped whirling and the dust they had

raised began to settle, he jumped out and came round to open her door.

Immediately the heat struck her like a blow from a clenched fist.

He took her hand to help her out.

She wanted him to keep holding it, wanted them to stay hand in hand. But, as soon as she was safely on the ground, he let it go and stepped back like a courteous stranger.

One of the hotel personnel was standing by and the two men exchanged a greeting and a few words in Italian before Zane turned to escort her through the green, leafy garden to the rear of the hotel.

As they climbed the steps to a vine-shaded terrace, where most of the tables were already occupied, a well-dressed elderly man came hurrying to meet them.

'Ah, Zane, how very nice it is to see you.' His English was good, but heavily accented.

'It's nice to see you, Pietro.'

They shook hands with great cordiality.

Then Zane said formally, 'Gail, I'd like you to meet Signor Boscolo, owner of the Firenzi... Pietro, may I present Signorina North.'

Liking the look of this pleasant, silver-haired man, she smiled and murmured a greeting.

Bowled over by that smile, he took her proffered hand and raised it to his lips with Latin gallantry. 'I am delighted to meet you, *signorina*. Zane has told me all about you. This is the first time you have visited our beautiful city?'

'Yes.'

'So after you have eaten lunch you will be going...how do you say...sightseeing?'

'I hope so.'

'Then I must not hold you up too long with talk.'

Turning to Zane, he went on, 'I have set aside for you a table on the terrace, but if you would prefer to eat indoors, you only have to say.'

After an interrogative glance at Gail, Zane answered, 'The terrace, please, Pietro.'

'A good choice on such a lovely day.'

Without further ado they were shown to a table for two in a secluded little arbour at the far end of the stone terrace. Shaded by vines, the perfumed air cooled by hidden fans, it was perfection.

When they were both seated, Pietro said, 'Today my head chef has excelled himself and I can highly recommend his Tonno Fresco alla Marinara, if the *signorina* likes fish.'

'Yes, I do,' Gail answered, and was awarded a beaming smile.

'In that case, may I suggest you start with Antipasto Volente and end with some truly delectable Cassata alla Siciliana?'

Both men waited for her decision.

Though she had little idea what any of the dishes were, she smiled and said, 'It all sounds delicious.'

Nodding to Pietro, Zane agreed pleasantly, 'Then we'll put ourselves in your very capable hands.'

'*Eccellente!* All you need now to complete your meal, which is…as you say…on the house?…is a good bottle of wine.'

They thanked him and he hurried away with yet another beaming smile.

Within seconds a wine waiter appeared with a bottle of perfectly chilled Orvieto and, after a nod from Zane, opened it and poured two glasses.

When the waiter had departed and Zane made no attempt at conversation, Gail took a sip of her wine and, needing something to say, asked, 'How long have you known Signor Boscolo?'

'It must be eight or nine years. He's Andrea and Paolo's uncle.'

'Oh,' she said in a small voice. She had been hoping to forget about Andrea for the next couple of hours. But, biting the bullet, she asked, 'Is that how you met her?'

'No, as a matter of fact it was the other way round. I first met Andrea and Paolo almost ten years ago when their parents took them to live in New York. Andrea was only nine, but Paolo and I were about the same age.

'Though they'd gone to join another branch of the family in a business venture that proved extremely successful, Catrina, their mother, was homesick, and none of them really settled.

'After coming back to Tuscany whenever possible to visit the rest of the family, last year they finally came home for good.'

So Zane had known Andrea since she was nine. That might explain why, that morning, he had from time to time treated her rather like a spoilt child.

At that moment their first course arrived and from then on, apart from an odd comment about the food, they both ate in a somewhat strained silence.

This wasn't how she had hoped it would be and, heavy-hearted, she realized that he'd been distant with her ever since she had rejected his kiss.

Oh, well, perhaps it was better this way. While there was this coldness between them, when the time came it might be easier to run.

The whole meal proved to be first class but, as far as Gail was concerned, she might as well have been eating chaff. It was a relief when coffee was served.

As soon as their cups were empty, they made their way into the hotel to say their thanks and goodbyes to Pietro Boscolo.

'You enjoyed the meal, I hope?' he asked anxiously.

They both assured him that they had, very much.

Obviously delighted, he clapped Zane on the shoulder. 'Not long to the wedding, eh? Will we see you before then?'

'I doubt it. We have a lot of places to visit in the next couple of weeks.'

'Well, if you *can* get over to Florence again, please do. It will be my pleasure to give you lunch.'

The last remark was addressed to Gail, whom he seemed to have taken a liking to.

As she murmured her thanks, he took her hand and added, 'If I don't see you before, we shall meet again at the wedding.'

Alerted by her expression, he asked quickly, 'You *will* be coming to the wedding?'

She said the first thing that came into her head. 'I haven't been invited.'

'Not invited! But you must come! I am sure Zane would want you there, and I know that any friend of his would be more than welcome. I'll mention it to Catrina without delay.'

'Th-thank you, you're very kind,' she stammered. 'But I really don't think—'

'Don't worry, I'll make quite sure she comes,' Zane broke in.

Gail cringed inwardly. Wild horses wouldn't drag her there, but of course he wasn't to know that. He no doubt assumed that their brief relationship was based purely on sex and meant as little to her as it did to him.

Which, in a way, was fair enough. But hadn't he considered his future wife's feelings?

A lot of the time, in spite of his powerful masculinity, he could be caring and sensitive, but when Andrea had been so blatantly angry and jealous of her, how he could be so unfeeling as to invite her to the wedding?

Knowing none of this, however, Pietro nodded and

smiled. 'Then I will look forward greatly to seeing you both on the day. Now, your car is waiting for you, so I will say *arrivederci.*'

'*Grazie…Arrivederci.*'

They left by the front entrance and, after the cool dimness of the air-conditioned hotel, the brightness was dazzling. The sun beat down, the air held a furnace heat and Gail could feel the stone slabs burning through the thin soles of her sandals.

A short distance away, a sea-blue open-topped two-seater was waiting, the keys in the ignition.

An elderly doorman, who had clearly been keeping an eye on the car, gave Zane a smart salute and opened the door.

'*Grazie tanto.*' Some folded notes changed hands.

As soon as Gail was settled in the passenger seat, Zane slid in beside her and a moment later they were pulling out of the forecourt to join the busy stream of traffic.

She hadn't expected them to go by car and she hoped it wouldn't hinder her chances of escaping.

After a while, afraid that if she didn't make some effort at normality Zane might suspect what was in her mind, she asked, 'What exactly are you planning to do?'

'As it's already mid-afternoon,' he said coolly, 'I think it makes more sense to leave the *palazzos* and museums et cetera for another time and just take a look at the main sights.'

Her heart sinking, she asked, 'You mean by car?'

He shook his head. 'No, bringing the car this far is just to save time. It's really not worth driving around central Florence. There's a one-way system that makes things difficult, and the historical hub of the city is closed to traffic.

'But I know somewhere we can safely park and then do some exploring on foot. Most of the things I was planning to show you are situated in the central traffic-free zone.'

He drove on and a little while later they came to a quiet, privately owned car park where, clearly well known, he was greeted by name and given a space in the shade.

From there they took a narrow *calle* and emerged on to a piazza surrounded by tall shuttered buildings, many with ornate wrought iron balconies.

In the centre of the piazza, almost deserted in the afternoon heat, there was a handsome marble fountain around which pigeons strutted and cooed and drank from water that had overflowed into a shallow basin.

They crossed the old square, walking a little apart like polite strangers, and a surreptitious glance at Zane's face confirmed that once again his expression was aloof, withdrawn.

Feeling an overwhelming sadness, she longed to slip her arm through his and see him turn and smile at her. Longed to get the feeling of closeness and intimacy back, to make the most of the short time they still had together.

But, reminding herself sternly that he belonged to another woman, she kept walking, staring straight ahead, blinking away the tears that threatened to blind her.

It would be as well if she could slip away as soon as possible. Delaying the moment of leaving him would only bring her more heartbreak.

But she must wait until they reached a spot where a lot of people were milling around. That way, as soon as his attention was elsewhere, it should be relatively easy to disappear into the crowd.

When she had regained control of her emotions and was reasonably sure her voice would be steady, she asked, 'Whereabouts are we starting?'

'At the Duomo,' he answered shortly. 'We'll be there in just a minute or so.'

The Duomo complex, with its cathedral, bell tower and octagonal baptistery, the exteriors of which were banded with green, white and pink Tuscan marble, was absolutely staggering.

'Compared with the outside, the interior of the Duomo is fairly austere,' Zane told her. 'But perhaps the relative bareness helps to make one appreciate the soaring space beneath the Gothic arches and the sheer scale of the place.'

They walked all the way round the cathedral so Gail could truly appreciate its vast proportions, before strolling down the Via dei Calzaiuoli which split the traffic-free area Zane had mentioned earlier.

In a short while they left the busy thoroughfare and branched off to look at some more of the city's glorious architecture.

After a couple of hours they stopped for a cool drink at La Cucina and sat in the open air beneath a gaily striped umbrella.

There was an entrance at either end of the café and a steady stream of waiters and people going in and out like ants.

When Zane called for the bill, seeing her chance, Gail excused herself on the grounds that she needed to wash her hands and freshen up and, heading for the nearest door, disappeared inside.

Making her way to the far door, she waited for a few moments until a small group was ready to exit, then slipped out with them. Only to find Zane had moved from the table and was stationed close by.

'That was quick,' he remarked blandly. Then, 'If you're feeling refreshed, shall we carry on?'

Though it was all quite fascinating, it came as something of a relief when they finally reached Piazza della Signoria, which marked the heart of the old town.

Gail was starting to feel hot and sticky and not a little concerned that, as if guessing her intention, Zane had scarcely taken his eyes off her.

When they had walked around Florence's main square and

admired the surrounding buildings, particularly the grand and austere Palazzo Vecchio and the many wonderful sculptures and statues, Zane asked solicitously, 'Tired?'

Scared that he was going to suggest going straight back to Severo, she said, 'A little, but I'm happy to go on if you are.'

He shook his head. 'I think we've done quite enough in this heat, so I suggest we call it a day and have dinner before going back to the car.'

Then, misinterpreting her anxious glance, 'Don't worry, we've circled round somewhat, so it's a lot closer than you might think.

'Now, is there anywhere special you'd like to go?'

There were many elegant cafés and smart restaurants scattered around the vast square and they all appeared busy. That was an important point, as this would almost certainly be her last chance to make a run for it.

As lightly as possible, she said, 'I don't really mind where we go. I'm happy to leave it to you.'

'In that case, we'll have a meal at Bartolomeo's. It's one of the least pretentious and the food is always excellent.'

If anything, Bartolomeo's was busier than the rest, but Zane was known there and welcomed with enthusiasm. The proprietor came hurrying out and, having shaken his hand, ushered them through a simple foyer and into a pleasant air-conditioned room.

There were no more than half a dozen widely spaced tables, all of which were occupied.

Snapping his fingers, Bartolomeo called an order and, while the two men exchanged a few words, a table for two was speedily set up in a flower-screened alcove by the window.

As Zane had said, the food was excellent and if Gail hadn't been so uptight and jumpy she would have thoroughly enjoyed the leisurely meal of Florentine specialities that followed.

Zane seemed to be waiting for her to speak. Gail, who could think of nothing to say, hoped he would put her silence down to tiredness.

They were sipping some excellent coffee before he roused himself to say, 'Before we venture out tomorrow, I'd like to do a little work on the Rainmaker project…'

It was the first time he'd mentioned work and, taken by surprise, she simply stared at him.

'What do you know about it?'

'W-well nothing really,' she stammered. 'Apart from the name.'

He nodded. 'My Research and Development team, who first came up with the revolutionary idea, named it that. They've been working on it for quite some time. But details of the project have been kept tightly under wraps because of the sheer amount of expertise and money that's already gone into it.

'Tomorrow, before we start work, we'll go through the plans together so you can see what I mean and get a good idea of exactly what's involved.

'However, the overall picture is this…'

Quickly and precisely, he explained what the project aimed to achieve both short-term and long-term.

Gail found it stunning in its scope and ingenuity and, with only Zane's brief account to go on, she could see that if it could be made viable it could bring prosperity to vast regions which at present wouldn't support life because of lack of rainfall.

'What a wonderful project,' Gail breathed.

'Isn't it? Of course there's a long way to go yet, but Rainmaker is the first step on the road.'

He poured them both more coffee.

While Gail sipped hers, she thought about what she'd just learnt. Now she had grasped just a little of what was involved, she knew—even without her change of heart—that she could never have helped Paul try to derail such a worthwhile project.

When their cups were empty, Zane observed, 'You're looking weary. About ready to go?'

She nodded and thought, *It's now or never...*

He called the waiter over and paid the bill before helping her to her feet and putting her light jacket around her shoulders.

They were on their way to the door when a tall, balding man rose from one of the tables and cried, 'Zane! It's good to see you, you old son-of-a-gun. What are you doing in Florence?'

Seizing the chance, Gail murmured, 'Excuse me,' and made her way through to the foyer and into the ladies' cloakroom.

She was hastily drying her hands and wondering if it was safe to make a run for it when the door opened and two elderly women dressed like well-to-do tourists came in chatting in English.

As soon as there was a pause in the conversation, Gail said, 'Excuse me, I know this sounds odd, but did you happen to notice a tall, good-looking man with dark hair waiting in the foyer?'

'I didn't,' the first one said. 'Did you, Isobel?'

'No.' Then, after a glance at Gail's face, 'I take it you're on holiday here and this is someone you're trying to get away from?'

'Yes, that's right,' Gail admitted.

Isobel nodded sagely. 'Some men can be perfect pests. If they buy you dinner they imagine they've bought you.

'Just a minute.' She opened the door and peered out cautiously, before reporting, 'Not a soul. Could he see the main exit from where he was?'

'Yes, I think so.'

'Then, just in case he's keeping an eye open for you, if you turn left when you go out of here, there's a side entrance that leads on to the patio. I know because we came in that way.'

'Thank you,' Gail said gratefully.

'Forgive me for asking, but if you leave alone have you enough money for a taxi back to your hotel?'

'Yes, I have, thanks.'

'Our husbands are waiting out there,' the first woman broke in, 'so if you think you might have a problem, stay with them until we come. Then we can all leave together.'

'I can't thank you both enough, but I'm sure if I can just slip out it'll be all right.'

'Take care now,' they said in a chorus.

Gail smiled and nodded. 'I will.'

The foyer was empty apart from a young couple who were just leaving and she was able to slip out through the side entrance with no trouble.

It was starting to get dusk but the lantern-lit patio was still busy, with waiters scurrying to and fro and new people arriving.

Having hurried across the piazza, she left the pedestrianized area and, hoping to spot a vacant taxi, made her way towards a road which was busy with evening traffic.

The one or two taxis she spotted were already taken and, though she had no idea where she was, afraid to stand still, she kept walking.

After fifteen minutes or so her luck changed. She was just passing what seemed to be a nightclub of some kind when a white taxi with a yellow design drew up by the kerb to drop its previous passengers.

Seeing her hovering, the driver, a bull-necked middle-aged man, leaned over and opened the door.

Thankfully, she climbed in.

Glancing at her, he asked laconically, *'Dove?'*

'I want to go to the airport,' she said, hoping against hope he would understand.

'Inglese, no?'

'Yes. I'm afraid I don't speak Italian.'

'Where you want to go?'

'The airport.'

'*Si, si...*'

Accompanied by hooting horns, colourful gesticulations and a veritable storm of abuse, he did what appeared to be an illegal U-turn and headed back the way she'd just come.

He seemed to speak a word or two of English, so she asked, 'How long will it take?'

She was beginning to think he hadn't understood, when he shrugged and said, 'Twenty minutes, *forse.*'

Not long. She breathed a sigh of relief. The sooner she was on a plane, the happier she would be.

As they headed through fairly heavy traffic, she wondered how Zane had reacted when he'd found she'd slipped away.

Had he just shrugged his shoulders and gone back to the car without her, or had he searched fruitlessly for her?

Given the circumstances, she rather thought it would be the former. A kind of easy come, easy go situation, where one woman meant little and there was always another waiting to fill the gap.

Would things alter when he was married? And if they didn't, would Andrea stand for it?

Gail strongly suspected that she wouldn't. She might turn a blind eye while they were merely engaged, but once she was his wife she would expect, and be entitled to, fidelity...

The journey to the airport was soon over and the driver dropped her outside the smaller of the two terminal buildings.

By the time she had paid him an exorbitant sum and thanked him, a group of four people were waiting to climb in.

When she made her way into the terminal building, she discovered she had been dropped—presumably because she had no luggage—at Arrivals.

The Departure terminal was larger and strangely quiet and,

on finding a female member of staff who spoke quite good English, she soon discovered that she was out of luck. The airport handled mainly domestic flights, with only a limited number of daily departures to other European cities.

Nothing could be done tonight, she was told, but tomorrow she would have the choice of either booking on a regular airline or going to Pisa, which was ninety kilometres from Florence and the region's main entry and exit point, especially for budget airlines.

Anxious and dispirited, she tried to decide what to do for the best.

After a moment or two's thought, she dismissed any idea of trying to get to Pisa. For one thing, it would probably cost more money than she'd got.

Which left her with two alternatives. She could take a taxi back to Florence and try to find a small hotel or she could stay where she was.

Feeling hot and sticky and tired out, she longed to shower and clean her teeth and stretch out in a proper bed. But the language barrier and the fact that she had no luggage suggested it would be a great deal easier to simply stay at the airport.

Most of the facilities seemed to be closed, but there was a deserted café-bar still open and, having bought herself a cup of coffee, she sat down at one of the small tables to decide once and for all what to do.

But, tired and dazed by lack of sleep, unable to concentrate, her thoughts kept swimming in and out of focus and, head drooping, all she could think about was Zane. Already she missed him.

Had she been wrong to leave him and run?

But what else could she have done? Cling to him until the very last minute? Make it so that he was forced to push her away? Or, worse, take her for his mistress, his plaything, while another woman reigned as his wife?

No, that would have been soul-destroying. An impossible situation. Tenable neither for herself nor for Andrea, should she ever find out.

Undoubtedly she had done the right thing. The only thing she could have done. Made a clean break.

Now she should be experiencing a feeling of release, a stirring of pride and self-respect that she had been strong enough to do it.

But she wasn't. In spite of everything, she longed for him, ached for him, felt the kind of pain that amputees were said to feel in limbs that were no longer a part of them…

Someone dropped into the vacant chair opposite, interrupting her sombre thoughts.

Her head came up and she found herself looking straight into Zane's glacial green eyes.

CHAPTER TEN

'W-WHAT are you doing here?' Gail asked stupidly.

Zane smiled without mirth. 'Surely you didn't think I'd let you go that easily?'

'But how did you know where to find me?'

'The airport seemed a pretty safe bet, and there are a lot of hotels in the city so it made sense to come here first.'

Smoothly, he added, 'Taxis are very expensive in Florence, but I presume you'd taken enough money to cover the fare?'

A hot flush staining her cheeks, she said, 'I didn't want to have to take it; it made me feel like a thief, but…'

As her words tailed off, he finished, 'But you had only a small amount of English money with you.'

'How do you know that?'

'While we were at your flat and I was waiting for you to finish packing, I went through your bag,' he admitted shamelessly.

'And you stole my phone!'

'I was merely taking care of it.'

'Why?'

'I would have thought that was obvious.'

'It's not obvious to me.'

'Think about it,' he advised sardonically.

Her fighting spirit up now, she said, 'I can't imagine why any normal boss should want to take his employee's phone.'

He smiled grimly. 'But there's nothing *normal* about our relationship, is there? Though you said you wanted the job, right from the start, and in spite of everything that's happened between us, or maybe *because* of it,' he added thoughtfully, 'you've been intent on running out.

'But after we showered together and you agreed to move into my room, I hoped things might have changed.' His gaze never left her for a second.

'It was only when we had our swim and I came back to find you in our bedroom and saw how guilty you looked that I knew they hadn't.

'All it needed was one look at your face to tell me what you'd been up to and what your intentions were.'

'Then I'm surprised you took your eyes off me,' she responded heatedly.

'I wouldn't have done if I'd thought you were still intent on running. But, having dangled the carrot, I fondly imagined you would stay to reap the reward…'

His words were like a kick in the solar plexus. But surely he couldn't have meant what, for one ghastly instant, she had thought he meant…

Pulling herself together, she said jerkily, 'I really don't know what you mean.'

'I'm quite sure you do. Now, if you're ready to go, I have the car waiting outside. We'll leave the chopper where it is and drive back to Severo.'

She shook her head. 'I'm going back to London as soon as I can get a flight.'

His voice cold, he told her, 'I'm afraid there's too much unfinished business between us for me to let you walk away scot-free.'

'U-unfinished business?' she stammered. 'What unfinished business?'

A hint of quiet menace in his voice, he said, 'No man in his right mind enjoys being made a fool of, but even that pales into insignificance compared to being deliberately betrayed.'

'Betrayed?' she whispered. 'But I haven't—'

'I'm quite sure you haven't. But I don't doubt that you would have done, given the opportunity.

'After all, wasn't that why you took the job as my PA—to be in a position to gather, and pass on, secret information?'

'I don't know what you're talking about,' she denied through stiff lips.

'May I suggest you give up on the injured innocent act. It doesn't cut any ice. Now, ready to go?'

Her hands clenched so tightly that she could feel the pain as the oval nails bit into her soft palms, she said hoarsely, 'I've no intention of going back with you.'

'Oh, but I insist. After all, what will your fiancé say if you let him down now after he's gone to so much trouble to set it all up?'

As she stared at him, aghast, he went on, 'Manton *is* your fiancé? It *is* his ring you were wearing round your neck?'

Knowing it was useless to deny it, swamped in cold despair, she asked, 'How long have you known?'

'From the word go.'

'Then why did you hire me?'

He smiled crookedly. 'Why do you think?'

Her tired brain struggled for a moment before the reason became blindingly clear. 'So you could get back at both of us… That's why you seduced me! You were planning to tell him, to gloat, hoping that it would wreck our engagement.'

'No, that wasn't the plan,' Zane said flatly. 'I've no inten-tion of telling him. In fact, as far as I'm concerned, your secret is quite safe.

'Of course, if you don't come up with the goods he may be angry enough to ask for his ring back…'

In a rush, she said, 'I have every intention of giving it back to him.'

'May I ask why?'

Biting her lip, she refused to answer.

Watching her face, he hazarded, 'A guilty conscience, perhaps, because you were a willing partner in this "seduction"?'

When she remained silent, he said, 'You'd be a fool to let it worry you. Manton is no saint.'

Infuriated by his careless dismissal of something that she still felt ashamed of, she hit back, '*You* might be totally without scruples when it comes to personal relationships, but that doesn't mean everyone is.'

His eyes narrowed. 'Perhaps you'd like to explain that remark?'

'I wouldn't have thought it needed explaining.' Then, in a rush, 'I can only feel sorry for Andrea.'

His eyebrows shot up. 'May I ask why?'

'She's obviously madly in love with you, and it must have been awful for her to find the man she's going to marry in a month's time playing around with another woman.'

After a moment he agreed solemnly, 'Awful indeed.'

'How *can* you be so callous, so uncaring?' she raged at him. 'Paul may be no saint, but he's twice the man you are.'

'In what way?'

'I'm quite aware that there have been women in the past, but he would never treat me like you're treating Andrea.'

'You think because he's given you a ring he's been faithful to you?'

She lifted her chin defiantly. 'I'm sure he has.'

Zane laughed. 'I don't like to burst your pretty bubble, but you're quite wrong.'

'Of course you would say that,' she cried, her voice full of contempt.

With a glance at his watch, Zane remarked, 'If he's not staying out too late I'd gamble pretty well everything I own that at this very moment he's in bed with another woman.'

As she opened her mouth to defend Paul, Zane went on, 'You don't have to take my word for it. Try ringing him and see what happens. You should be able to tell from his reaction whether or not you've caught him out.'

'You took my phone.'

Reaching into his pocket, he brought out his mobile and offered it to her. 'You can use mine.'

When she hesitated, he asked, 'What's the matter? Scared I might be proved right?'

'No, I'm not. But the whole thing seems…I don't know… wrong, distasteful.'

He shrugged. 'Well, of course I could have been misinformed, but you'll never be sure if you don't give it a go.'

Seeing her waver, he suggested, 'Tell me the number and I'll get it for you.'

She gave him Paul's home number and watched him key it in.

'If it bothers you,' Zane went on, 'don't think of it as possibly catching him out. Just tell him what kind of mess you're in and see what he says.

'Perhaps he'll saddle his white steed and come charging to the rescue.'

Angered by his mockery, she took the phone and listened to the number ringing.

She was just about to give up when the receiver was lifted and a sleepy female voice mumbled, 'Hello?'

Without conscious volition, Gail found herself asking, 'Is Paul there?'

'He's asleep. Can't it wait until morning…? Oh, very well… Paul… Paul… Wake up… Some woman wants to speak to you…'

Feeling curiously numb, uncaring, Gail pushed the *end call* button and handed back the phone. After a moment, she asked dully, 'What made you so sure?'

'My detective told me Manton had a woman living with him and has had for some time. I thought at first it was you, but then he showed me a photograph he'd taken of them leaving the apartment together early one morning.

'Though it was only taken with a phone, it was good and clear. It seems Manton's taste runs to tall, curvaceous blondes…'

Then he wasn't on his own, Gail thought bitterly.

Watching her face, Zane said with a hint of genuine sympathy in his voice, 'I'm sorry if it's come as a shock to you, but I couldn't see the point of letting you live in a fool's paradise.'

He was right, of course, but knowing made her feel both hurt and angry. Hurt that Paul had just tried to use her, and angry that she had allowed him to.

But she recognized that it was her pride that was hurt rather than her heart. And the fact that the engagement had been merely a ploy made her feel a lot less guilty about her own actions.

So she had escaped lightly.

Or had she?

There was still Zane to answer to and he wasn't the kind of man who would easily forgive what he clearly regarded as treachery.

But what could he possibly do to her if she stayed where she was and refused to leave the airport?

Nothing, surely?

Though she still felt scared, even her fear seemed less sharp, blunted by tiredness.

Pressing her fingertips to her throbbing temples, she wished fervently that he would just go and leave her in peace.

Exhausted, both by the heat and the roller coaster of emotions she'd ridden all day, the only thing she wanted at that moment was to be left alone. She longed to fold her arms on the table, lay her head on them and simply close her eyes.

Watching her face, he said, 'It's been a long day and you look shattered. You should be on your way home to bed.'

'I'm staying here.'

'That's where you're wrong.' Taking her elbows, he lifted her to her feet.

'I won't go back,' she insisted, trying in vain to free herself. 'If you don't let me go, I'll scream blue murder.'

When he made no attempt to release her she took a deep breath, but before she could carry out her threat he pulled her into his arms so that she was off balance and his mouth came down on hers, stifling any attempt to cry out.

Holding her tightly, he kissed her until she was dazed and breathless, then asked softly, 'Ready to admit defeat?'

'You can't make me leave,' she said huskily when she'd managed to regain her balance. 'Someone is bound to realize that something's wrong.'

'Don't bet on it. Italians tend to be hot-blooded, romantic, and to an outsider this will appear to be just a lover's tiff.'

'I'll tell them I'm being kidnapped.'

He laughed. 'How do you plan to do that when you don't speak the language?'

'There's someone here who understands English.'

'Where?'

Gail looked around but there was no sign of the woman she had spoken to earlier and, apart from a sleepy-looking youth who was in the process of closing down the bar, a couple of female cleaners and, in the distance, a security guard, the terminal appeared to be deserted.

'Please, Zane,' she begged jerkily. 'Don't make me go back.'

Just for an instant his expression softened. Then it hardened again and he said grimly, 'Manton may have put you up to this in the first place but, to put it bluntly, you're the one on the spot and I want…' He paused.

White to the lips, she whispered, 'Revenge?'

'Let's call it recompense.'

Handing her her bag, he urged her towards the exit.

Though she strongly suspected that he could well be both cruel and ruthless, beaten, defeated, bone weary, she allowed herself to be shepherded out of the building.

Outside, it was a lovely moonlit night. There wasn't a soul in sight and everywhere seemed to be quiet as the grave. The car, its top closed now, was waiting nearby in the pick-up area.

As soon as she was seated, he slid in beside her and fastened both their seat belts. A second or so later, with a muted roar, they were underway.

Almost before they had left the airport environs, she was sound asleep.

She had no recollection whatsoever of the journey. The first thing she knew was fingers stroking her cheek and Zane's voice saying, 'We're home.'

She opened her eyes and, trying to fight off the relentless waves of sleep that threatened to engulf her, struggled out of the car.

He helped her across the courtyard and into the house, but her legs were like a rag doll's and already her leaden eyelids were starting to close.

She felt herself lifted in strong arms and, her head pillowed comfortably against his shoulder, she gave up the fight and let herself sink back into the blessed oblivion of sleep.

When she opened her eyes it was broad daylight and she was alone in the big bed. Still partially entangled in the golden cobwebs of sleep, her mind was blurred, hazy, anything but clear.

Yet she felt a foreboding, a sense of anxiety and loss she couldn't immediately account for.

Then memory opened the curtains a crack.

Zane was planning to get married and, because she couldn't bear to stay, she had managed to give him the slip and run.

But if she had run away, what was she doing here in his bed?

Almost immediately the curtains were swept aside.

Zane had caught up with her at the airport. He knew that she had been intending to spy for Paul and, intent on punishing her, he had made her come back with him.

She could recall nothing of the journey and had only the vaguest recollection of arriving back and being carried upstairs to bed.

But she was naked, so he must have undressed her, and the dent in the other pillow confirmed that during the night he had slept beside her.

Now it was day and quite soon, no doubt, she would have to face him and answer for what she'd done.

Not that she had actually *done* anything. But Zane would no doubt say that the intention had been there. And perhaps it had, just briefly.

Though she knew now that even if Zane had been ignorant of her role as a spy, and the opportunity had arisen to pass on the information Paul had wanted, she couldn't have gone through with it.

But she would never be able to convince Zane of that in a million years.

Though it was warm and the room was filled with sunshine, she began to shiver.

A glance at the bedside clock showed it was nearly midday.

She had slept for almost twelve hours, and she felt unrefreshed and apprehensive.

What she needed was to brush her teeth and shower.

Emerging from the bathroom some fifteen minutes later, physically refreshed but even more apprehensive about what lay ahead, she pulled on clean underwear and a light cotton dress before brushing out her long seal-dark hair.

Leaving it loose and still slightly damp, she gritted her teeth and made her way downstairs, telling herself that it was better to face him than have him come looking for her.

Dressed in casual trousers and a short-sleeved olive-green shirt, he was just emerging from the morning room.

As always, her heart turned over in her breast at the sight of him.

Considering that he'd had a great deal less sleep than she'd had, he appeared to be the picture of health and vitality. His clear green eyes were brilliant, his lean tanned face looked alert and dangerously attractive.

'Good timing,' he greeted her mildly. 'I was just coming to see if you were still asleep. Lunch is waiting on the terrace. You must be hungry.'

Trying for normality, she agreed, 'I am, rather.'

'I'm afraid you'll have to put up with my cooking again,' he went on smoothly. 'I gave Maria the day off so we could have a little…privacy.'

'You're trying to scare me,' she accused.

Hearing the quaver in her voice, he observed with satisfaction, 'I appear to be succeeding.

'But there's no need to look like a frightened rabbit.'

Anything but reassured, she preceded him on to the sunny terrace and sank down in the chair he pulled out for her.

As he sat down opposite her and reached to pour her a

coffee, wanting to get the whole thing over with, she took a deep breath and began, 'Zane, I'm sorry I—'

'May I suggest we eat lunch first,' he broke in coolly, 'and leave any apologies and explanations until later.'

They ate chicken, fresh bread and crispy salad without speaking. A tense silence hung in the air.

Gail refused the fruit and cheese that followed, but accepted another cup of coffee.

'It's getting very hot in the sun,' Zane remarked. 'Shall we move into the shade to drink our coffee?'

They moved to chairs where the wisteria above them cast shadows on to their bare arms, making strange tattoos of flowers and leaves.

Her coffee finished, Gail put her cup on the low table and, realizing that Zane was waiting for her to speak, deliberately remained silent.

After a little while he smiled that wolfish smile. 'But a rabbit with attitude, I see… Now, if I remember rightly, you were about to apologize.'

Wanting to say, *Apologize be damned,* but knowing it would be useless to fight him, she said simply. 'Yes, I was.'

'And you'd like me to forgive you?'

'I'd like you to believe that if I'd been given all the information Paul wanted, I would never have passed it on.'

'I do believe it.'

She made a little sound, almost like a sob of relief. Then she said passionately, 'I never wanted to get involved in the first place, and when I was offered an interview I was…'

'Hoping you wouldn't get the job,' he finished for her. 'That was fairly obvious. You couldn't hide your relief when you thought you hadn't.

'But at the same time you didn't want to let Manton down

so, when I finally offered you the post, you felt forced to take it. Though you clearly weren't a happy bunny.

'I got the distinct impression that you were planning to tell Manton what a swine I'd been to you, in the hope that he'd let you off the hook…'

So that was why he'd taken her phone.

'But it would have been a complete waste of time. He wasn't likely to relent, having set everything up so carefully.'

'When did you find out?' she asked breathlessly.

'Some time ago, Moira, my ex-PA, suspected what was afoot and warned me.

'She and a woman named Julie, who went to the same gym, had become friendly. But Moira's no fool and it didn't take her long to realize that whenever my name was mentioned, Julie was pumping her for information.

'Then she discovered that her new friend was Manton's sister, and told me about it.

'Manton had already managed to plant one spy but, because we'd rumbled her, she must have proved to be virtually useless.

'When I checked things out it soon became obvious that he was planning to try again with someone closer to the action.' He paused to sip his coffee, then went on.

'I hired a good detective to keep an eye on his comings and goings and who he was associating with. As soon as I had all the gen, and knew who he was hoping to set up as my new PA, I decided to facilitate matters.'

'Facilitate matters…?'

'I told Mrs Rogers that when Manton approached her, she was to agree to send Miss North for an interview straight away.'

'So you knew who was coming before I got there?'

'Oh, yes.'

'When you knew the whole thing was a set-up, I don't understand why you chose to see me, let alone offer me the job…'

'I thought you'd decided it was so I could get my own back by breaking up your engagement?'

'But if you knew Paul had another woman and didn't care a jot about me, that theory doesn't make sense.'

Brushing that quibble aside, Zane said, 'Tell me, how did he manage to pressure you into doing something you clearly didn't want to do?'

When she didn't immediately answer, he said, 'I presume he made it a test of your devotion?'

'Yes,' she admitted wearily.

'You must have loved him very much.'

'At the time I thought I did.'

For what seemed an eternity, Zane sat without moving a muscle.

Then he took a deep breath and asked carefully, 'What about now?'

'I realized I'd been mistaken about my feelings.'

'Presumably that was last night when you found he'd only been using you?'

'No, I knew before then that not only had I never loved him, but I'd never really liked him. It was just a kind of infatuation.'

'Then why do you look so lovelorn?'

Startled, she said, 'I don't…' Then, more positively, 'I'm not.'

'Pity. I was rather hoping…'

Letting the words tail off, he remarked, 'You don't seem to have much luck with the men in your life.'

Pulling herself together, she protested, 'You make it sound as if there've been dozens.'

'I know about Jason and Manton. How many others have there been?'

She hesitated, then, not wanting him to know just how lonely and barren her adult life had been, said, 'A few…'

'Lovers?'

'Just casual friends.'

'The sort of casual friends you go to bed with?'

'No, I don't make a habit of going to bed with my men friends.'

'Presumably you went to bed with Jason?'

She shook her head.

'You're not telling me he didn't try?'

'No. He tried too hard. I was fond of him, but I didn't love him and I didn't want to go to bed with him. That's why we broke up.'

'So you'd only go to bed with someone you loved?'

Realizing she'd walked into his trap—if it *was* a trap—she froze.

But he merely said, 'So that just leaves Manton.'

'Apart from a few kisses, he never as much as touched me.' Her little smile held a tinge of bitterness. 'I wasn't aware he had a woman living with him, so I stupidly put it down to him having good old-fashioned principles.'

'The kind you were brought up with?'

Suspecting derision, she said coldly, 'I know it's unfashionable, laughable even, but I—'

He held up a restraining hand. 'Believe me, I'm not knocking it. I'd like the woman I marry to have those kind of principles.'

'I'm sure she has,' Gail said stiffly.

His handsome green eyes brilliant, he studied her heart-shaped face with its high cheekbones, neat nose, generous mouth and beautiful almond eyes beneath dark silky brows, before saying reflectively, 'There's something I'm curious about.'

'What's that?'

'You indicated just now that you would only go to bed with someone you loved…'

Seeing where that was leading, she said hastily, 'Or someone I was very strongly attracted to.'

'So you were very strongly attracted to me?'

'W-well, yes.'

'On your own admission, I seem to have been the only man you've been "very strongly attracted to", so how do you explain the fact that, though you were evidently inexperienced, you weren't a virgin?'

Her face scarlet, she took refuge in anger. 'I don't have to explain. It's none of your business.'

'Oh, but I rather think it is…

'Let me tell you a story. Seven years ago, when I was young and foolish, I fancied myself in love with a glamorous blonde whose name was Rona…'

Watching the colour drain from Gail's face, leaving it petal-pale, he went on, 'She and her family—her American father, English stepmother and young stepsister—lived in New York.

'As well as being glamorous, she was smart, sexy, uninhibited and fun in bed. Yet I always thought that, like a spoilt child, she had a certain vulnerability.

'She seemed to be what I was looking for and I was all ready to propose when I discovered that I'd been just a stopgap while she tried to find a man with more money.

'You've heard the expression, Don't shoot the messenger? Well, in my case I did. That is to say I took my anger and disappointment out on an innocent young girl who, fancying she was in love with me, attempted to console me.

'I've never forgiven myself for that.

'Later the same evening, I went round to the apartment block where she lived. I had intended to tell her how sorry I was for being such a brute and beg her forgiveness.

'However, circumstances gave her a chance to get a little of her own back, and I spent most of the evening trying to convince the police that I wasn't some kind of criminal.

'Do I need to go on?'

'No,' she whispered. Then, hoarsely, 'I'm sorry. I shouldn't have done it, but I was hurt and angry—'

'And you had every right to be. Though just then I was too furious to take that into account.

'Then next day when I'd cooled down, I made another attempt to see you, only to be told that both you and your mother had packed your bags and gone.

'Rona's father said he'd no idea where you'd gone or why you'd left. I had a nasty feeling it was because of me, and I felt even worse.'

Gail shook her head. 'Though I was only too glad to leave New York, it wasn't because of you. My mother wanted to get away…'

Briefly she explained where they'd gone and what had happened to make her mother finally decide to end the marriage.

'I'd no idea things were so bad,' Zane said soberly, 'and as no one was sure whether you'd gone for good, for several weeks I kept calling, hoping you might have returned.

'When she discovered I knew the truth, Rona admitted that the weekend on Chator's yacht had proved to be a disaster. I gather she had unexpected competition—three in a bed.

'She said she was sorry she'd lied to me, and swore she still loved me. She wanted things to carry on as if nothing had happened…'

'And did they?'

He shook his head. 'There's a lot to be said for being totally disillusioned. It removes the rose-coloured spectacles, makes one able to walk away. I realized I had a lot to thank you for.'

She looked up at him with wide, innocent eyes. 'Then you're not still mad at me?'

'No. But I'm still sorry for the way I treated you. It could have put you off men for life…

'Perhaps it did… Have you really loved any man?'

Only one.

When she said nothing, he pressed, 'Have you?'

She shook her head silently. Then, needing to change the subject, she asked, 'When did you realize who I was?'

'When my detective showed me a photograph of you. I could hardly believe my eyes. I'd been trying to find you for seven years.'

'I'm surprised you still recognized me.'

'Though you've grown up and matured, and the colour of your hair has changed, I could never forget those eyes. They're the most beautiful eyes I've ever seen on a woman, and they've haunted me.'

Some impulse at self-flagellation made her say, 'Andrea has beautiful eyes, don't you think? In fact, she's a beautiful woman altogether.'

'I totally agree. With that perfect oval face, the long blonde hair and big brown eyes, she's grown up to be a stunner. It's just a pity she's not my type.'

'Not your type!' Gail sat up, shocked.

'No, I much prefer a woman who has a heart-shaped face, hair like black silk, clear, dark grey almond eyes, with an even darker ring round the irises, and a wide, passionate mouth.'

Trembling all over, she demanded, 'Then why are you marrying Andrea?'

He laughed softly. 'I'm not.'

'But she talked about having a dress made for her, about you and she being together in church…'

'That's right, but the dress that's being made for her is a bridesmaid's dress, and we'll be in church together because I'm the best man.'

'Then who's getting married?'

'Moira, my ex-PA, and Paolo. They first met a couple of

years ago in New York and became friends. Then friendship blossomed into romance, and in a month's time they'll be man and wife.

'Andrea was highly delighted when the pair got engaged, and offered to help them with the wedding plans. She was even more pleased when Paolo asked me to be his best man.

'Though there's a big age gap, she fancied she was in love with me and, in spite of getting no encouragement, I think she's been cherishing hopes that one wedding might lead to another.'

'Poor thing,' Gail murmured, feeling sorry for the other girl.

'Don't worry, it won't last long,' he said confidently. 'In a few months' time she'll have transferred her affections to, hopefully, a more grateful recipient.'

He leaned across and, taking her hands, pulled her out of her chair and on to his lap, cradling her to him.

His lips against her temple, he murmured, 'You see, unlike you, my constant nymph, she's always been a butterfly child.

'You once said you loved me. It's my hope and belief that you love me still, and I want to hear you say it…'

He hadn't said he loved her and, while she would have given everything she owned to hear him say those three words, what he had said would have to do.

Turning her head to look into his face, she told him, 'I loved you then and I love you now. I've never stopped loving you.'

'That's good, because if you didn't love me I don't know what I'd do.

'For seven long years I've tried to find you and for all that time you've haunted me. I couldn't get you out of my mind or my heart.

'Then, when I finally found you again and I thought you loved Manton, I nearly went mad with jealousy.'

His face pressed against her throat, he whispered, 'You'll

never know how much I've longed to hold you in my arms. To kiss your lips and wipe out the past. To tell you how very much I love you, and to ask you to be my wife.'

When, too full to speak, she sat in a blissful silence, he said anxiously, 'You will, won't you?'

Making up her mind to tease him a little, she queried, 'Will what?'

'Be my wife?'

'I'll have to think about it.'

'*Think* about it?' he echoed in mock outrage.

'I'll need to know just what kind of husband you'll make before I say yes.'

'What if I promise to be sober and upright…?'

'Well, that's a start.'

'Generous, caring and faithful?'

'Even more important…' Then, softly, she asked, '*Will* you be faithful?'

'Do you doubt it?'

'No.'

'Good.' He kissed her. 'Now, where was I? Oh, yes, I promise to always stay by your side, to love and cherish you and keep you happy in every way…?'

'Can you promise things like that?'

'Why not? Loving and cherishing go hand in hand, and I could no more stop loving you than I could stop breathing. And, as for the rest, I know of at least one way I can keep you happy…'

'Oh, what's that?'

'In bed.'

'I see,' she said demurely.

'So what do you think?'

'I'm starting to think that marrying you might not be a bad idea. Though, before I finally say yes, you might need to refresh my memory on that last score.'

Standing up with her cradled in his arms, he kissed her and said, 'My love, I would say "the pleasure's all mine" except that I prefer that kind of pleasure to be shared.'

Passion, love and marriage with these powerful Sheikhs from our bestselling authors

18th July 2008

15th August 2008

19th September 2008

17th October 2008

Collect all four!

M&B

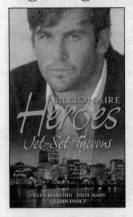

Celebrate 100 years of pure reading pleasure with Mills & Boon®

To mark our centenary, each month we're publishing a special 100th Birthday Edition. These celebratory editions are packed with extra features and include a FREE bonus story.

Plus, you have the chance to enter a fabulous monthly prize draw. See 100th Birthday Edition books for details.

Now that's worth celebrating!

July 2008

The Man Who Had Everything by Christine Rimmer
Includes FREE bonus story *Marrying Molly*

August 2008

Their Miracle Baby by Caroline Anderson
Includes FREE bonus story *Making Memories*

September 2008

Crazy About Her Spanish Boss by Rebecca Winters
Includes FREE bonus story
Rafael's Convenient Proposal

Look for Mills & Boon® 100th Birthday Editions at your favourite bookseller or visit www.millsandboon.co.uk

4 FREE

BOOKS AND A SURPRISE GIFT!

We would like to take this opportunity to thank you for reading this Mills & Boon® book by offering you the chance to take FOUR more specially selected titles from the Modern™ series absolutely FREE! We're also making this offer to introduce you to the benefits of the Mills & Boon® Reader Service™—

- ★ **FREE home delivery**
- ★ **FREE gifts and competitions**
- ★ **FREE monthly Newsletter**
- ★ **Exclusive Reader Service offers**
- ★ **Books available before they're in the shops**

Accepting these FREE books and gift places you under no obligation to buy, you may cancel at any time, even after receiving your free shipment. Simply complete your details below and return the entire page to the address below. You don't even need a stamp!

YES! Please send me 4 free Modern books and a surprise gift. I understand that unless you hear from me, I will receive 6 superb new titles every month for just £2.99 each, postage and packing free. I am under no obligation to purchase any books and may cancel my subscription at any time. The free books and gift will be mine to keep in any case.

P8ZED

Ms/Mrs/Miss/Mr ....Initials ....
BLOCK CAPITALS PLEASE

Surname...

Address...

....

....Postcode...................................

Send this whole page to:
UK: FREEPOST CN81, Croydon, CR9 3WZ